WORLD GONE QUIET

C. D. REEVES

To my wife and two incredible children,
who ensure I never feel alone in this vast world.

Part 1	**1**
1	3
2	11
3	18
4	25
5	32
6	38
7	44
8	50
9	61
Part 2	**69**
10	71
11	77
12	82
13	88
14	93
15	99
Part 3	**107**
16	109
17	113
End	**119**

PART 1

Bernie was a simple man. He lived alone—utterly, achingly alone, in a way that pressed against his chest like a weight he couldn't shift. There wasn't another soul left to share the silence with, not a single voice to break the stillness that had settled over the world like a thick, unyielding fog. No animals, either—not a chirp, not a rustle, not even the hum of an insect to interrupt the quiet. He enjoyed cooking, or at least he told himself he did. It was a ritual, a tether to something human when everything else had slipped away. He'd wander out to the tangled patch of earth behind his house, where wild onions sprouted in stubborn clumps near the river's edge. Their green shoots poked through the cracked soil, defiant little survivors in a world that had given up. He'd kneel, his knees sinking into the damp ground, and dig them out with a rusted trowel he'd found years ago in someone else's shed. The toxic, earthy scent made his eyes water as he crushed them into a paste with a flat river stone, his hands moving with the slow, deliberate rhythm of habit. Later, he'd mix the paste into whatever he'd managed to forage that day —maybe a handful of bitter roots he'd pried from the dirt with cracked fingernails, or a few shriveled berries from a thorny bush upstream. He was a vegetarian now, not by choice but by necessity. There was nothing else. No fish in the rivers, no rabbits in the fields, no birds in the sky. Just plants, tough and sparse, clinging to life as stubbornly as he did.

He cooked over a fire he built in the crumbling hearth of what used to be his house. The chimney had collapsed long ago, leaving a pile of crimson bricks and a gaping hole in the roof where the smoke curled upward in lazy spirals, disappearing into a sky that seemed too vast, too empty. The flames flickered against the blackened stones, casting shadows that danced across the walls —walls that were peeling now, their faded paint curling away like dead skin. He'd sit there, cross-legged on the floor, watching the roots soften or the berries stew, the heat prickling his face. It wasn't much of a meal, but it was enough to quiet the gnawing in his gut. The silence pressed in as he ate, unbroken by any sound beyond the crackle of the fire and the faint whistle of wind through the broken roof. He'd grown used to it, or as used to it as a man could get.

When the light faded and the world turned quiet— quieter than it had any right to be—he'd pick up his ukulele. It was a battered thing, its wood chipped and sun-bleached from years of neglect, but it had four strings and a subtle way of giving the silence a voice. He'd found it in the wreckage of a neighbor's house, back when he still bothered to explore the ruins, and he'd kept it ever since. He'd carry it out to the sagging porch steps, the boards creaking under his weight, and settle there as the last streaks of daylight bled into the horizon. His fingers, rough and calloused, would pluck at the strings, coaxing out soft, aimless tunes that floated into the emptiness. The notes didn't echo anymore—not like they used to, when there were walls and windows and people to catch the sound and toss it back. Now they drifted, fragile and fleeting, swallowed by the vast, silent nothing that stretched beyond his little patch of earth. It relaxed him, or at least it kept his hands busy so his mind wouldn't wander too far into the places he didn't want to go.

It had been years since it all happened. So many he'd stopped counting, stopped marking the passage of time with anything more than a vague sense of *before* and *after*. It gets harder to count the years when you stop counting the sunsets, when the days blurred into one long, unbroken smear of orange and gray and shadow. He didn't have a calendar anymore—didn't need one. What was the point when every day was the same? Wake up, eat breakfast, get his work done, go home, sleep. Same routine, different day. The sun still rose each morning, painting the sky with hues that felt wasted on a world with no one left to see them. The river still flowed, its waters churning over rocks worn smooth by time, but its surface felt flat and lifeless, reflecting nothing but the sky above. His stomach still growled when he didn't feed it. Small constants in a world that had lost its shape, its purpose.

The next morning began like all the others. Bernie woke to silence that was broken only by the faint creak of the cot as he shifted his weight. He lay still for a long moment, sprawled on the portable bed he'd dragged into the corner of the living room years ago. His eyes traced the cracks in the ceiling, jagged lines that spread like veins across the plaster, illuminated by the pale light seeping through the gaps in the boarded-up window. There was no sound to greet him—no chirping, no rustling, just the hush of a world emptied out. He'd once taken noise for granted, back when the air was thick with it: the growl of car engines, the chatter of voices, the electric hum of a world that buzzed with life. Now there was nothing, and the absence was a weight all its own. He wondered, as he often did, how long he could stand it—the silence, the solitude, the sheer *nothingness* of it all.

He rolled out of bed, his joints complaining like the old floorboards beneath his feet, and shuffled to the kitchen—or what passed for one now. The room was a shell of its former self: the cabinets hung open, their doors long gone for firewood; the sink sat dry and rusted, its pipes useless without running water. A dented aluminum pot rested on a makeshift table of stacked cinder blocks, its surface scratched and blackened from years of use. He filled it with water from a plastic jug he'd hauled up from the river the day before, the liquid sloshing against the sides with a faint, hollow sound. Then he reached into a burlap sack hanging from a nail on the wall and pulled out a handful of dried berries —small, shriveled things he'd scavenged last week from a thorny bush a mile upstream. They were tart and tough, but he tossed them into the pot to soften them anyway, watching them bob on the surface like tiny, dark islands. Breakfast. Nothing fancy, nothing to write home about—if there'd been anyone left to write to. He ate standing up, leaning against the wall, his gaze drifting out the window to the overgrown yard beyond.

The grass out there was chest-high now, a wild, tangled sea of green and brown, dotted with dandelions and thistles that swayed in the breeze. It had swallowed the old flowerbeds Ellen used to tend, the ones she'd filled with marigolds and daisies back when color meant something. Beyond the yard, the road stretched out, its asphalt cracked and buckled, weeds pushing up through the fissures like they were reclaiming it inch by inch. It disappeared into a haze of dust and memory, leading nowhere now. Bernie chewed slowly, the berries sticking to his teeth, and let his eyes linger on the emptiness. He didn't look at the houses anymore, the ones that lined the old street. Their windows were dark, shattered panes staring blankly at nothing; their doors hung open, swaying faintly in the wind like mouths frozen mid-scream. He'd stopped going inside them years ago. There was nothing left to find—no people, no animals, just dust and decay.

Many years ago, Bernie had a job just like any other man. Nothing special, nothing that would've made him stand out in a crowd, but it paid the bills. He'd been a mechanic, working in a garage on the edge of the city—a squat, concrete building with a flickering neon sign that read "Marty's Auto Repair." He could still smell it sometimes: the tang of gasoline, the greasy bite of motor oil, the faint metallic scent of tools scattered across the workbench. His hands had been stained black back then, the grime worked so deep into his skin it never really came out. Every two weeks, he'd get a paycheck, a thin slip of paper he'd cash at the bank downtown. It supported the family—him, Ellen, Sarah. He could still hear them if he let himself: Ellen's laugh, friendly and bright as a bell, cutting through the evening air; Sarah's small fingers tugging at his sleeve, her voice soft and insistent, *"Daddy, tell me a story."* He'd regularly think to himself, *How pointless was all that?* The grinding hours under car hoods, the petty arguments with customers over a few bucks, the endless cycle of work and sleep and starting over. He hadn't known what pointless really meant until it was all stripped away.

When everything happened—whatever *it* was—the world didn't end with a bang or a scream. It just… stopped. One by one, the lights went out, the voices faded, the cities emptied. The animals went too—birds falling silent, fish vanishing from the waters, every living thing winking out until only buildings and plants remained, tenacious and mute. Bernie didn't know why he'd been spared, if you could call it that. Maybe it was luck. Maybe it was punishment. Either way, he'd learned just enough "real world" skills to get by after the event. How to dig roots from hard soil. How to filter river water through layers of cloth and charcoal. How to tell which plants wouldn't kill him—the hard way, once or twice, with nights spent curled up in agony from a bad choice. He'd never been a survivalist but necessity had a way of teaching fast, of carving lessons into your bones.

Work today meant foraging along the riverbank. He grabbed his walking stick—a gnarled branch he'd worked smooth —and stepped outside. The air was cool and heavy, thick with the scent of damp earth and the faint, sour rot of decaying wood. He moved slowly, picking his way through the tall grass, his boots crunching on gravel that had spilled from the road years ago and now lay scattered like forgotten confetti. The river glittered in the distance, a silver ribbon cutting through the ruins of what used to be, its surface seemingly unmoving under the morning sun. He followed the overgrown path he'd worn over time, his steps steady but unhurried, his breath fogging faintly in the chill.

He stopped at a patch of ground where he'd spotted some edible roots the day before—tough, fibrous things that grew deep and required effort to unearth. He knelt, digging with the trowel, the soil crumbling under his hands. The roots came up in clumps, dirt clinging to their pale, twisted forms. He brushed them off and slipped them into the canvas sack slung over his shoulder. It wasn't much—barely a meal—but it was something. He straightened up, wiping his hands on his patched trousers, and paused. For a moment, he thought he heard something—a rustle, a whisper—but it was just the wind moving through the reeds, their dry stalks clattering faintly against each other. He shook his head, a faint grimace tugging at his lips. He was always hearing things these days, ghosts of sounds that weren't there, echoes of a world that had moved on without him.

Back home, he rinsed the roots in river water and set them to cook over the fire, the flames crackling as they softened the tough fibers. The smell drifted through the house, earthy and faint, a small comfort in the emptiness. He sat back on the porch steps, the ukulele in his lap, and watched the sky deepen from gold to violet, the colors bleeding together like a painting no one would ever see. Another day done. Another sunset he didn't bother to count. He plucked a few notes, letting them drift into the stillness, their soft twang swallowed by the night. He wondered—not for the first time—how long he could keep this up, how long he could live in a world that had forgotten how to live.

He didn't have an answer. He never did.

Bernie's memory was foggy, a haze of half-formed shapes and whispers that slipped through his fingers like smoke. What really happened that day—the day everything stopped? He sat on the edge of his cot, elbows resting on his knees, staring at the warped floorboards beneath his boots. The wood was splintered and gray, worn smooth in places by years of his pacing, his solitary footsteps the only mark left on it. Did he ever actually have a family? He could picture Ellen's face sometimes—her blue eyes crinkling at the corners when she smiled, her hair falling in loose waves over her shoulders—but the image flickered, unsteady, like a reflection in a rippling puddle. Sarah, too, appeared at the edges of his mind: a small, hazy figure with a high giggle, always willing to dance. Were they real, or had he conjured them from the emptiness, a desperate trick to fill the void? Did he really work that 9-to-5, hunched over engines in a greasy garage, the hum of machinery vibrating through his bones? He could still feel the weight of a wrench in his hand, the ache in his back after a long shift, but the details were hazy—dates, faces, the name of the boss who'd barked orders over the roar of the shop. Was he ever a child, running through summer grass, chasing shadows under a sky that wasn't yet so heavy? Or had he always been this —alone, ageless, a man unmoored from time?

Lack of human contact could do that to a man, he supposed. No touching, no talking, no eyes to meet his and say, "You're here. You're real." It was through others that we knew ourselves, a mirror of existence held up by the presence of someone else. Take out the other half of the equation, strip away the voices and hands and beating hearts, and what was left? Did he really exist, or was he just a shadow moving through a world that had forgotten him? He rubbed his palms together, the calluses rasping faintly, and felt the warmth of his own skin. It was something, a small proof, but it wasn't enough. His thoughts circled, chasing their own tails, and found no answers. The silence pressed in, thick and unrelenting, a companion he hadn't asked for but couldn't shake.

All Bernie really knew for sure was that he was alone. As far as he could tell, not one other living thing had survived in this world—no animals to stir the stillness, no birds to break the sky with their wings, no fish to ripple the rivers. Just him and the unwavering plants that pushed up through the cracks in a planet that had gone quiet. He'd walked miles in every direction over the years, his boots kicking up dust on roads that led nowhere, his eyes scanning the horizon for any sign of life. He'd found nothing but ruins and weeds, the skeletons of trees clawing at the air with bare branches, their leaves long gone. The world was a graveyard of itself, and he was its only mourner.

The city he'd once called home laid to the east, a sprawling expanse of concrete and steel that had once thrummed with life. He remembered it—or thought he did—bustling with noise and motion: cars honking, radios blaring, people shouting over the clatter of footsteps on crowded sidewalks. Now it was dark, its towers leaning like tired giants, their windows shattered into jagged maws that swallowed the light. Vines crept up the sides of buildings, their tendrils curling through broken bricks, and the streets were choked with weeds that split the pavement apart. One man could only do so much, and Bernie had given up trying to hold it together long ago. The decay had won, spreading like a slow tide, and he'd let it. He didn't go there anymore unless he desperately needed a change in scenery. He didn't like the way the silence felt in a place that had once been so loud. It was disturbing, unnatural—a hush that screamed louder than any noise ever had.

He'd retired himself to his old house instead, a modest two-story relic in a suburb just beyond the city's edge. The familiarity of it was a comfort, or at least as close to comfort as he could get. The street outside was lined with other houses, their roofs sagging and lawns swallowed by wild grass, but his was the only one he'd bothered to claim. The walls were weathered, the paint peeling in long, curling strips, and the windows were now just shattered holes. Inside, the air smelled of dust and damp wood, a faint mustiness that clung to everything. The furniture was sparse—a cot in the living room, a rickety chair by the hearth, a table of cinder blocks—but it was his. He could handle the silence here, in a place where he'd once known the creak of every step, the way the light slanted through the kitchen at noon. It was a ghost of a life he might have lived, and that was enough to keep him anchored.

Bernie did enjoy the night sky, though. Since the lights in the city had gone out, flickering off one by one until the grid was nothing but a memory, he'd gained a whole new respect for the dark. He'd step out onto the porch after dinner, a ritual in itself, and tilt his head back to look up. The stars were sharper now, unblurred by the haze of civilization, spilling across the black in a dazzling sprawl he'd never noticed before. They glittered like shards of glass, cold and distant, but alive in a way the earth no longer was. "Stars can't shine without darkness", he thought, and the darkness here was absolute. No streetlights, no headlights, no glow from a neighbor's window—just the vast, unbroken night stretching out forever. It was beautiful, in its way, and it made him feel small but not entirely alone. The night sky was the one thing that hadn't changed, the one thing that didn't care he was the last.

It had taken him many years to notice the faint light in that sky, or maybe it just appeared, a pinprick of something different amid the familiar constellations. He'd been sitting on the porch one night, the ukulele idle in his lap, when his eyes caught it—a soft, pulsing glow, barely brighter than the stars around it. At first, he'd dismissed it as a trick of his vision, a tired mind playing games in the dark. He'd squinted at it, his eyes tired in the dark, and felt a flicker of curiosity stir in his chest—something he hadn't felt in years. What was it? A plane, frozen in time? A satellite, still orbiting a dead world? He had no idea, and he let it be. Curiosity was a luxury he couldn't afford, not when every day was a battle to keep going. Even as Bernie opted to shift his focus to the rhythm of the steady pluck of the ukulele strings, the light stayed. He didn't know then how that simple glow in the night sky would, one day, mean everything.

For now, everything in Bernie's world seemed to be on repeat. Wake up, eat breakfast, forage, cook, sleep. The same steps, the same motions, day after day, etched into his bones like a script he couldn't rewrite. He'd start each morning by hauling water from the river, the plastic jug heavy in his hands as he trudged back up the path he'd worn through the grass. The water was clear but lifeless, its surface undisturbed by anything but the wind. He'd filter it through a scrap of cloth and a handful of charcoal he'd made from burned wood, then boil it in the dented pot over the fire. Breakfast was whatever he'd scavenged the day before—maybe a handful of sour berries, or a few tough roots he'd dug up near the riverbank. He'd sit on the porch to eat, the sun climbing slow and indifferent overhead, and watch the world do nothing. The grass didn't rustle with hidden life; the trees didn't sway with the weight of unseen creatures. It was just him and the empty world, locked in a quiet, unchanging dance.

After breakfast, he'd set out to forage, his walking stick tapping against the ground as he moved through the suburb. The houses around his stood like silent sentinels, their yards overgrown with thistles and dandelions, their porches sagging under the weight of time. He'd check the spots he'd marked in his mind—places where edible plants still grew, stubborn patches of green in the gray. Today, he headed toward an old garden a few streets over, its wooden fence collapsed into a heap of splinters. The soil there was dry and hard, but he'd found a cluster of wild carrots once, their thin, pale roots a rare treat. He knelt, digging with the trowel, the dirt crumbling under his hands. The carrots were still there, stunted but edible, and he pulled them free, brushing off the soil with fingers that trembled faintly from the effort. He slipped them into his sack, the canvas rough against his knuckles, and stood, his knees popping like dry twigs.

The walk back was slow, the sun beating down on his shoulders, the air heavy with the scent of dust and decay. He passed a playground he'd avoided for years, its swings hanging motionless, their chains rusted into stiff curls. The slide was cracked, half-buried in weeds, and the sandbox was a shallow pit of grit. He didn't look at it long; it reminded him too much of Sarah—or the idea of her—laughing as she slid down, her hair flying behind her. Real or not, the memory hurt, and he turned away, his stick tapping a steady rhythm against the ground.

Back home, he cooked the carrots over the fire, their faint sweetness mingling with the smoky air. He ate in silence, the crackle of the flames his only company, then carried the ukulele out to the porch. The sky was darkening, the stars emerging one by one, and there it was again—that faint, pulsing light. He watched it in his subconscious as he played, his fingers moving over the strings in time with its rhythm, a quiet duet in a world that offered no response. The notes drifted out, thin and lonely, and he felt something in him shift, a slow unraveling he couldn't name.

When you take out the randomness of other life—people, animals, the chaos of a world in motion—you begin to shut down. Bernie felt it happening, piece by piece. His thoughts grew sluggish, his movements mechanical, his days bleeding into one another until they were indistinguishable. He was shutting down, folding in on himself like a flower with no sun to turn toward. The light in the sky was a curiosity, a question, but it wasn't enough—not yet. For now, he was a man alone, repeating the same steps, waiting for something he couldn't define.

He set the ukulele down, the last note fading into the dark, and stared at the pulsing glow. How long could he keep this up? How long until the shutdown was complete?

He didn't know. He never did.

Many months had passed, each one bleeding into the next until they were a shapeless smear of time. Bernie was so close to giving up, the weight of it pressing down on him like a stone he couldn't shift. There was no purpose in life anymore, nothing to live for—no voices to call his name, no hands to pull him forward, no reason to keep dragging himself through the endless cycle of days. He'd kept going out of habit, a stubborn reflex carved into his bones, but even that was wearing thin. The world was a hollow shell, its silence a relentless mirror reflecting his own emptiness back at him. He'd stopped counting the sunsets long ago, stopped caring whether the sun rose or fell, because it didn't matter. Nothing did.

Tonight, he lay sprawled on the roof of another empty building, one of the countless husks that dotted the city's decaying landscape. He'd climbed up here in desperation for any kind of change, his boots scuffing against the rusted fire escape, his hands gripping the cold metal rungs until he hauled himself onto the flat expanse of concrete. The roof was littered with debris —broken glass glinting faintly in the starlight, a tangle of wires from some long-dead antenna, a scattering of dry leaves that crunched under his weight. He'd settled onto his back, the roughness of the surface digging into his spine through his patched jacket, and stared up at the star-ridden sky. It stretched above him, vast and unbending, a tapestry of pinpricks that shimmered against the black. The air was cool, tinged with the faint, acrid scent of rust and rot, and it brushed against his face as he lay there, eyes wide open, tracing patterns he'd memorized years ago.

That's when he noticed it again—the different light in the sky. It wasn't like the stars, with their faraway, twinkling edges. This one had a pulse, a soft, rhythmic glow that waxed and waned like a heartbeat, steady and deliberate. It seemed closer than a star, its light less piercing, more diffused, but not bright enough to rival the moon—which hung pale and lifeless overhead, a silent witness to his solitude. He couldn't tell its distance, couldn't judge how far it hung above the earth, but he knew it was beyond his reach, its source too distant to hear or touch. He'd seen it before, that faint anomaly, but tonight it held his gaze, pulling at something deep inside him—a thread of curiosity he thought he'd lost. His breath slowed, fogging faintly in the night air, and he watched it pulse, a quiet rhythm against the chaos of his thoughts. Exhaustion crept in, heavy and insistent, and his eyelids drooped despite himself. He fell asleep there on the roof, the concrete hard against his back, the pulsing light the last thing he saw as the dark took him.

When he woke the next morning, the sky was a pale, washed-out gray, the stars faded into the creeping light of dawn.

His body ached, stiff from the cold and the inflexible surface, and he sat up slowly, rubbing at his eyes with the heels of his hands. The memory of the light lingered, intense and vivid, but doubt crept in alongside it. Had he imagined it? Maybe it was a dream, a trick of a mind too long left to wander alone. He squinted up at the sky, now empty of anything but the sun's faint glow, and shook his head. Dreams were all he had left to fill the silence— dreams of Ellen's kiss, Sarah's small hands, a life that might never have been real. A pulsing light could easily be another illusion, another ghost conjured from the void. He climbed down from the roof, his boots clanging against the fire escape, and trudged back to his house in the suburb, the question gnawing at him but unanswered.

Some time later—he couldn't say how long, days or weeks lost to the blur—he saw the light again. He'd been on the porch, the ukulele resting in his lap, his fingers idle on the strings as he stared out into the night. The stars were there, as always, but so was the pulse, faint and steady, cutting through the familiar pattern. He sat up straighter, his breath catching, and watched it. It wasn't a dream this time; he was awake, his senses sharp, the wood of the porch beneath him grounding him in the moment. Over the next few nights, he kept looking, and it kept appearing —not every night, but often enough to make him wonder. It wasn't until the seventh viewing, weeks later, that he realized it was real. He'd climbed onto the collapsing roof of his own house this time, a vantage point he rarely used, and lay there with his hands behind his head, the torn shingles rough against the back of his hands. The light pulsed above him, undeniable, a rhythm he couldn't ignore. It wasn't a star, wasn't a trick of his eyes. It was *something*, and that certainty settled into him like a stone dropping into still water.

Then Bernie started studying. He needed to understand it, to make sense of the one thing in his world that didn't fit the endless desolation. He created a schedule, a purpose he hadn't had in years. He scavenged a scrap notebook from the wreckage of a neighbor's house—the kind you would use for taking notes in school, its edges yellowed and curling—and a stub of pencil he'd kept in a drawer. He marked the nights he saw the light, scratching faint lines and numbers in the dim glow of his fire. He'd sit on the porch or climb to the roof, his eyes fixed on the sky, waiting for it to appear. Some nights it didn't, and he'd sit there until the cold drove him inside, his eyes squinting in the dark, his hands clenched around the ukulele he no longer played. Other nights, it pulsed into view, and he'd note the time— guessing from the position of the moon and stars, the only clock he had left. He tracked its schedule, its comings and goings, and slowly, a pattern emerged. It wasn't random; it had a schedule of its own, a cadence he could predict if he watched long enough.

The act of observing gave him something to hold onto, a thread of meaning in the unraveling fabric of his days. He'd wake each morning with a flicker of purpose, his routine shifting to accommodate this new task. He'd haul water from the river as always, the jug heavy in his hands, the path through the grass worn deep by his steps. He'd forage for roots and berries, his trowel digging into the hard earth, his sack filling with the tough, sparse bounty of a world without life. But now, as he worked, his mind turned to the light—what it might be, why it was there, how long it had been pulsing unnoticed above him. He cooked his meals over the fire, the flames crackling in the hearth, and ate quickly, eager to finish so he could climb to the roof or step onto the porch and watch. The stars became his map, the pulsing light his compass, and for the first time in years, he felt a spark of something like hope—or at least the shadow of it.

But he was afraid, too. Humans have an innate nature to fear what they don't understand, and Bernie understood nothing about this light. Was it a remnant of the world before, a machine still ticking in the void? Was it something new, something watching him as he watched it? The thought sent a shiver through him, cold and piercing, and he began to observe in shadow. He'd tuck himself against what was left of the chimney on the roof, its crumbling bricks shielding him from view, or sit just inside the doorway on the porch, the darkness cloaking him as he peered out. He could see the light, but he didn't know if it could see him —if it had eyes, if it cared. The idea of being seen, after so long alone, was both a longing and a terror. He'd spent years invisible, a ghost in his own world, and the thought of something breaking that solitude made his heart stutter.

Weeks passed, then months, and the rhythm solidified. The light appeared on nights only Bernie could predict, pulsing for hours before fading as the sky lightened. He'd mapped it out in his notebook, the pencil marks smudged but legible, a fragile record of his discovery. He knew when it would come now, could count the days and be ready. And that's when he decided: he would show himself when the time was right. He'd step out of the shadows, stand in the open, and really face it—whatever it was. The idea took root slowly, growing through the cracks of his fear, until it felt inevitable. He'd spent too long hiding, too long shrinking into himself. If the light was a sign, a signal, a chance at something more, he had to take it.

What did he have to lose? Nothing. He'd lost it all already —family, friends, a world that made sense—or maybe he'd never had it to begin with. His life was a loop of survival, a threadbare existence stitched together with routine and silence. The light was a break in that pattern, a question he couldn't ignore. If it was nothing, if it meant nothing, he'd be no worse off than he was now. But if it was *something*—if it held even the smallest promise of meaning—he had to know. He had to try.

The night he chose came after days of preparation, though there was little to prepare. He'd washed his face in river water, scrubbing at the grime with his hands, and smoothed his tangled hair as best he could. He'd patched a new tear in his finest jacket with a scrap of cloth, threading a needle he'd found in Ellen's old sewing kit—or what he remembered as hers. He ate early, a handful of bitter roots softened over the fire, and climbed to the roof as the sky darkened. The stars emerged and he waited, his breath shallow, his hands trembling faintly at his sides. The light appeared on schedule, pulsing softly, and he stood, stepping out from the shadow of the chimney into the open expanse of the roof.

He faced it, his silhouette stark against the concrete, his eyes locked on the glow. "I'm here," he whispered, his voice hoarse from disuse, barely audible over the wind. He didn't know if it could hear him, didn't know if it mattered. But he stood there, exposed, a man alone under a sky that might finally see him.

And he waited.

The anticipation swelled in Bernie, a tight, unfamiliar knot in his chest that pulsed with every beat of his heart. It had been so long since he'd had anything to look forward to—years, decades maybe, lost to the gray fog of survival—that he'd almost forgotten what it felt like. The sensation was raw, electric, a mix of hope and dread that prickled along his skin like static. Good or bad, something was about to happen, and it all came down to this moment, this night, this rooftop where he stood alone under the vast, indifferent sky. He'd stepped out from the shadow of the broken down chimney, his silhouette stark against the broken shingles, his boots planted firm as if rooting him to the earth, and addressed the sky. The pulsing light hung above, faint but steady, a rhythm he'd memorized over months of watching. "I'm here," he whispered again, his voice rough and thin, barely cutting through the stillness. He cleared his throat, louder now, and said, "I'm here." He tilted his head back, eyes wide, and stared directly at the light, giving it his undivided attention—every ounce of his will, his being, poured into that gaze. "I'm here!" he cried out.

But the light didn't respond. It pulsed on, stubborn and unchanged, as if he were nothing more than a speck in the vast expanse of a world that had forgotten him. The wind tugged at his jacket, a faint howl rising from the city below, but the sky remained silent. Maybe it wasn't enough. Maybe standing there, a lone figure on a crumbling roof, was too small a gesture to pierce the distance between him and whatever that light was. Maybe it needed more—a bigger show, a louder cry—to see him amid the emptiness that stretched out in every direction. His shoulders slumped, the anticipation souring into a dull ache, and he lingered there a while longer, staring until his eyes burned and the cold seeped into his bones. The light pulsed on, oblivious, and finally, he turned away.

He climbed off of the roof and shuffled back inside his house. The familiar mustiness greeted him—dust and damp wood, the scent of a place left to rot. He sank onto the cot, the springs groaning faintly, and lay there, staring at the cracked ceiling. Disappointment gnawed at him, a quiet sting that settled deep, but it didn't break him. Not yet. He wasn't defeated; he was too stubborn for that, too tethered to the flicker of purpose the light had sparked in him. As he drifted toward sleep, his mind churned, grasping for something more, something foolproof. And then it came to him—a crude, reckless plan, born from the haze of exhaustion and desperation. If the light could see anything at all, it would *have* to notice this. His lips twitched, a ghost of a smile, and he slipped into the dark with the idea burning bright in his mind.

The next morning, he woke with an even greater sense of purpose, a fire kindled where only embers had smoldered before. The sky was a flat, pale gray, the sun a muted glow behind a shroud of clouds, but he didn't care. He rolled off the cot, an unexpected excited motion, and stood, stretching the stiffness from his limbs. His plan was simple but massive: he'd gather anything flammable—gasoline, alcohol, hairspray, whatever he could find—and turn the city into a beacon the light couldn't ignore. When you're the only one left, the supplies run deep, scattered across a world that no one else claims. The city was a treasure trove of abandoned things, relics of a life that had stopped, and he'd plunder it all to make himself seen.

He started that day, stepping out into the brisk morning air with his canvas sack slung over his shoulder and his walking stick tapping against the ground. The suburb lay quiet around him, its houses slumped under the weight of time, but he headed east toward the city, where the buildings loomed taller and the streets held more promise. His boots crunched on gravel and broken glass as he crossed the boundary where the suburb gave way to urban decay—a line marked by a toppled street sign, its letters faded to illegible smears. The city sprawled before him, a labyrinth of concrete and steel, its towers leaning like weary sentinels, their windows dark and jagged. Vines snaked up their sides, weeds choked the pavement, and the air carried the faint, sour tang of rot. He didn't linger on the silence here, didn't let it unsettle him as it once had. He had work to do.

His first stop was a gas station on the outskirts, its pumps rusted and dry, but the underground tanks were another story.

He'd found them years ago, still half-full of gasoline, preserved by the lack of anyone to siphon them dry. He pried open the access hatch with a crowbar he'd scavenged from a hardware store, the metal screeching in protest, and lowered a battered bucket tied to a rope. The fumes hit him first, searing and heady, stinging his eyes as he hauled up the dark, sloshing liquid. He poured it into plastic jugs he'd collected over time—old water bottles, bleach containers, anything with a cap—and sealed them tight, stacking them in a cart he'd rigged from a shopping trolley and some scavenged wheels. It took hours, his arms aching, his breath short, but he filled a dozen jugs before the cart was full. He wiped the sweat from his brow, the gasoline's scent clinging to his hands, and moved on.

Next, he hit the residential blocks, weaving through streets lined with apartment buildings and brownstones, their doors hanging open like invitations no one would take. He climbed decrepit stairs to dusty bathrooms, rifling through cabinets for hairspray cans, their nozzles still primed with flammable mist. He found bottles of rubbing alcohol, their caps cracked but contents intact, and tucked them into his sack alongside half-empty cans of paint thinner from a garage down the street. Every find fueled him, each clink of glass or hiss of aerosol a step toward his goal. He worked until the sun dipped low, then hauled his trove back to the suburb, the cart rattling behind him over the uneven ground. It was just the beginning.

In the months that followed, Bernie turned his plan into a fevered obsession. He scoured the city day after day, his steps purposeful, his eyes on the lookout for anything that could burn.

He raided a liquor store, its shelves still lined with bottles of whiskey and vodka, their amber contents gleaming in the dim light. He broke into a pharmacy, smashing the glass counter to reach cleaning supplies—ammonia, bleach, anything volatile he could use. He even ventured to an industrial district on the city's edge, where he found a warehouse stacked with propane tanks, their metal surfaces dulled by dust but heavy with promise. He rolled them out one by one, the effort leaving him breathless, and dragged them back in trips that stretched over weeks. His hands blistered, his back screamed, but he didn't stop. The light pulsed in his mind, a rhythm he couldn't shake, driving him forward.

The real prize came when he remembered the mine miles down the road—a quarry he'd passed years ago, its entrance half-collapsed but still accessible. He trekked there one morning, the sun barely up, and squeezed through the narrow gap, his flashlight cutting through the dark. Inside, he found crates of dynamite, their sticks wrapped in faded paper, the fuses brittle but intact. He handled them gingerly, his heart thudding, and carried them back in small batches, sweat beading on his forehead as he navigated the rocky path home. It was dangerous, reckless, but that was the point. The world hadn't seen this much devastation in years—not since it all stopped—and he'd make it see again.

Bernie placed his flammable findings throughout the city with meticulous care, turning it into a tinderbox ready to ignite. He soaked carpets in buildings with gasoline, the liquid glugging from his jugs to seep into the fibers, the fumes thick and dizzying. He carefully placed propane tanks for the biggest bang, craving those moments of shock and awe. He trailed lines of alcohol along hallways, the fumes mixing with the dust, and tucked dynamite into corners where it would amplify the chaos. He worked in silence, the city's hush unbroken by anything but the slosh of liquid and the clank of metal, his hands steady despite the tremble in his chest. It took months, maybe years, his days consumed by the labor, his nights spent planning the next move. He'd stand on rooftops sometimes, surveying his work, the skyline a patchwork of decay and potential fire. His only hope was that the light would recognize his efforts, that it would see the blaze and know he was here.

The thought was somehow satisfying, a dark thrill that coiled deep inside him. Deep down, we all crave destruction, he mused— the urge to tear down, to break apart, to leave a mark that can't be ignored. More importantly, we all want to be noticed, to have our existence etched into something bigger than ourselves. He'd been invisible too long, a ghost drifting through a dead world, and this—this inferno he was building—would be his shout into the void. The light had ignored his whisper, his quiet stand on the roof, but it couldn't ignore a city ablaze. Nothing could.

He felt a sense of completion on a night when the air was still, the sky clear, the stars a backlit canopy with holes punched in it. Bernie stood on the roof of a high-rise in the city's heart, the tallest he could climb, its cracked concrete ledge overlooking the streets he'd primed. He'd hauled up a final jug of stale gasoline, its weight pulling at his arms. The pulsing light was there, right on schedule, its glow faint but steady above him. He set the jug down, his breath shallow, and pulled the notebook from his pocket—the schedule he'd scratched out long ago, smudged but legible.

He was almost ready.

5

For his final preparation, Bernie had found a truck—an old, rusted hulk abandoned on the city's edge, its faded red paint flaking away to reveal the dull steel beneath. It sat in a weed-choked lot near the industrial district, its tires sagging but still clinging to their rims, a relic of a world that no longer moved. He'd spent a day wrestling with it, prying open the hood with a crowbar until the hinges screeched, and coaxing the engine back to life. His hands, stained with grime, fumbled with wires and a scavenged battery until it sputtered awake, coughing black smoke into the still air. The giant gas tank was his prize, a cavernous reservoir he filled to the brim with gasoline hauled from his earlier scavenges—jugs he'd lugged over in his rattling trolley, pouring until the fumes burned his throat and the liquid sloshed against the sides. Then, with a hammer and a nail he'd found in the truck's toolbox, he'd punched a hole in the tank's underside, a jagged tear that leaked fuel in a slow, deliberate drip. He climbed into the cab and drove it back to his house in the suburb, the engine growling low as it trailed a glistening "fuse" of gasoline along the road—a dark, shimmering line stretching from the city's heart to his doorstep, a promise of fire waiting to be kept.

He would light this fire to watch the city burn, a final, roaring act to shatter the silence that had entombed him for years. And if the light in the sky witnessed it—if it saw the inferno he'd crafted with nothing but sweat and will—maybe he'd finally be worthy of meeting whatever it was that pulsed in the dark, watching him from a distance he couldn't cross. The thought consumed him, a feverish blend of longing and resolve, as he pictured the flames tearing through the streets he'd primed. He saw it in his mind's eye: the low-rise apartments igniting first, their gasoline-soaked carpets flaring into walls of orange and gold, the heat shattering windows into glittering shards that rained onto the pavement below. The propane tanks he'd strategically placed would burst, sending shockwaves through the night, plumes of fire and smoke spiraling upward to claw at the stars. The taller buildings would follow, the ones he'd laced with dynamite and drenched in alcohol, their collapse a symphony of destruction—booms and cracks and the shriek of twisting metal as the city's bones broke apart. The skyline would glow, a jagged crown of flame against the black, a beacon no light could ignore. It was a vision that fueled him, a promise of chaos and recognition, and he clung to it like a lifeline.

It was time.

That night, Bernie sat straight up in his bed, the cot's springs groaning under the sudden shift. The room was dark, the air thick with the musty scent of dust and damp wood, but his pulse hammered in his ears, the perfect tempo of anticipation. He swung his legs over the side, his boots thudding against the floorboards, and reached for the box of matches he'd scavenged from one of the city's many bars—a small wooden thing he'd found behind a counter, its label peeled away but the matches inside still dry and eager. He slid it into his pocket, the faint weight of it grounding him, and grabbed his jacket from the chair by the hearth. The fabric was patched and fraying, but it would shield him from the night's chill. He stepped outside, the air brushing his face like a whisper, and set off toward his fuse, his walking stick tapping a steady rhythm against the gravel-strewn path.

It was a dark night, the kind that swallowed everything beyond arm's reach. The clouds had vanished, leaving the sky bare and black, but the moon was a thin crescent, its light too feeble to pierce the gloom. The stars glittered above, beautiful and unknowing, a vast canopy that seemed to press down on him with its indifference. Bernie knew the mysterious light would appear soon, right on schedule, its pulse cutting through the familiar sprawl of constellations. He'd tracked it long enough to predict its rhythm, to know it would linger for hours—plenty of time to set the city ablaze, to send his message roaring into the void. His breath was steady as he walked, the gasoline trail glinting faintly under the starlight, a dark ribbon winding from his house toward the city's edge. He followed it, his steps slow but resolute, the anticipation tightening in his chest with every yard.

He reached the spot where the trail widened, where he'd parked the truck days ago just beyond the suburb's boundary. The leaking tank had left a puddle of fuel soaking into the earth, a slick, dark pool that shimmered faintly in the dim light. He knelt beside it, the sharp scent of gasoline filling his lungs, a heady sting that made his eyes water. His hands trembled—not from doubt, but from the sheer weight of the moment—and he pulled the matchbox from his pocket, sliding it open with a soft rasp. He counted the sticks inside: thirteen, their red tips lined up like soldiers ready for battle. He set them on the ground beside him, then leaned back on his heels, his gaze lifting to the sky. The stars stared back and he waited, the silence wrapping around him like a shroud.

In that stillness, his mind drifted to the fire he'd unleash. He imagined it racing along the fuse, a serpent of flame leaping from the truck to the city, hungry and unstoppable. The suburb would fall first, its sagging houses catching like dry tinder, their peeling walls swallowed by the blaze. The fire would surge onward, crossing the boundary into the city's streets, where he'd soaked carpets and packed rooms with volatile treasures. He saw the low buildings flare up, their interiors igniting in a rush of flame and light, the propane tanks he'd placed bursting in deafening explosions that would shake the ground beneath his feet. The taller towers would follow, the dynamite he'd tucked into their corners detonating with a force that would split concrete and hurl debris skyward, a rain of ash and sparks against the night. The warehouse on the industrial edge would erupt last, its stockpile of fuel and explosives a final, cataclysmic roar that would paint the horizon red. Smoke would rise in thick, choking spirals, blotting out the lower stars, and the city would burn—a molten heart pulsing in time with the light above, a scream he'd carved into the world with his own hands.

He lingered on that vision, the destruction unfolding in vivid detail behind his closed eyes. The heat would reach him here, a dry wind searing his skin, the roar of it drowning out the silence that had haunted him for so long. The skyline would twist and buckle, a jagged silhouette of flame and ruin, and the light— the light—would have to see it. It would have to see him. He pictured it flaring in response, its pulse quickening, a sign that his act had pierced the distance between them. Or maybe it would descend, drawn by the chaos, a glowing answer to the question he'd burned into the earth. The thought sent a shiver through him, a mix of fear and longing, and he opened his eyes, his breath shallow, his hands steadying against the ground.

He didn't have to wait long. He'd light the fuse as soon as it appeared—just as he'd planned, just as he'd promised himself. His gaze swept the sky, searching, his heart thudding against his ribs. And then... it was there. As suddenly as ever, cutting through the dark with its faint, pulsing glow. It hung low, dimmer than the stars but very much present, its rhythm steady and deliberate, a heartbeat against the stillness. Bernie's eyes locked onto it, his pulse syncing with its own, and he felt a jolt— a certainty that it was staring back at him, watching from the night sky with an intent he couldn't grasp. His lips parted, a whisper slipping out: "I'm here." The words faded into the air, but they were irrelevant. The light was his witness now, and he'd make sure it saw everything.

He struck the match.

The small stick flared to life with a hiss, a bright tongue of flame dancing at its tip, casting flickering shadows across his face. He held it, the heat prickling his fingers, and stared at the pulsing light one last time, his breath held tight in his chest.

6

Bernie was ready. He stood beside the truck, the gasoline-soaked ground glinting faintly under the starlight, his boots planted firm in the dirt. The match flared in his hand, a small, trembling flame that cast a warm glow across his weathered face, its hiss a faint counterpoint to the silence that enveloped him. He looked at it, the fire gyrating at the tip, and waited—two full seconds, a deliberate pause before the act that would change everything. The night stretched around him, dark and vast, the thin crescent moon hanging low, its light too weak to compete with the stars that glittered above. The air was cool, tinged with the subtle bite of gasoline fumes, and it brushed against his skin as he held the match steady, his breath fogging in the chill.

In those couple of seconds, doubt crept in, swift and cold, threading through his resolve like a crack in glass. What if the light was all in his imagination? The thought struck him hard, a whisper from the depths of a mind too long left to wander alone. It wouldn't be the first trick his solitude had played on him. He'd seen shadows move in empty houses, heard voices in the wind— Ellen's laugh, Sarah's soft pleas for a story—only to turn and find nothing but dust and decay. His memory was a fog, a tangle of half-truths and ghosts, and the light could be another illusion, a desperate hope conjured from the void. Those two seconds stretched, heavy with uncertainty, and he stared at the match, its flame flickering as if it, too, questioned his intent. The city waited beyond, primed with his endless labor—gasoline-soaked carpets, propane tanks, dynamite—a tinderbox he'd built to scream into the silence. But what if there was no one to hear it?

He lifted his gaze to the sky, the match still burning in his hand, and found the mysterious light where it always appeared—low and faint, pulsing with its steady rhythm against the black. It was there, as real as the ground beneath him, or so he'd convinced himself. The doubt lingered, a shadow at the edge of his mind, but he pushed it aside, focusing on the glow that had become his anchor. He stared at it, willing it to see him, to prove it wasn't just another trick. The match's temperature grew, prickling his fingers, but he barely noticed, his attention locked on the light. And then, suddenly, it changed.

The light in the sky, usually so faint it could be mistaken for a distant star, erupted with fountains of bright white light. It flared, a sudden, dazzling burst that spilled across the night, easily ten times brighter than the moon's pale sliver. Bernie's breath caught, his eyes widening as the glow intensified, radiating outward in shimmering waves that pulsed faster, stronger, a heartbeat turned to a drumroll. It bathed the world below in an unearthly brilliance, casting strange shadows down upon the deserted city. The buildings—crumbling husks of concrete and steel—seemed to dance in the night, their jagged outlines twisting and swaying as the light shifted, playing across their surfaces like a living thing. The vines that clung to their walls stood out in stark relief, their tendrils curling like frozen fingers, and the cracked streets gleamed, the gasoline trail reflecting the glow in a shimmering line that snaked toward the horizon.

Bernie stared, transfixed, his mouth dry, his pulse hammering in his ears. The match burned on in his hand, its flame a pitiful flicker against the radiance above, but he'd forgotten it entirely. The light was no illusion—it was real, and it was responding. The realization hit him like a wave, washing away the doubt that had gripped him moments before. The city didn't burn, not yet, but it didn't need to. The light had seen him. He wasn't as alone as he'd once thought, and that in itself—a single thread of connection in a world stripped bare—inspired him to continue. His chest tightened, a mix of awe and relief swelling within him, and he stood there, bathed in the glow, a man no longer invisible.

The match scorched his fingers, a sudden, stinging pain that snapped him back to the moment. He cursed, dropping it to the ground, where it sputtered and died in the dirt, a faint wisp of smoke curling upward. He shook his hand, the sting fading as he flexed his burned fingers, but his eyes never left the light. It pulsed on, brighter than he'd ever seen it, a beacon that cut through the dark. He rubbed his hand against his jacket, the rough fabric smooth against his skin, and let the truth settle into him: the light didn't want to see the city burn. It had flared at the very moment he'd held the match, a reaction too precise to be chance. It had been watching him all this time—every night he'd tracked it, every step he'd taken to build his fire—and it had chosen this moment to answer.

But why? The insistent question that bloomed in his mind as he stood there under its gaze. Why had it watched him, silent and distant, for years? Why had it waited until now, until he'd stood poised to set the world ablaze, to show itself? He tilted his head back, the light's brilliance stinging his eyes, and searched its glow for meaning. Was it a machine, a remnant of the world before, orbiting a dead planet out of habit? Was it something else —something alive, something aware, drawn to the last man standing in a sea of nothing? He had no answers, only the weight of its presence, a mystery that pressed against him as heavily as the silence once had.

He stepped back, his boots crunching on the gravel, and sank onto the truck's hood, the metal a welcoming cool beneath him. The city sprawled before him, untouched by fire but transformed by the light, its shadows shifting as the glow pulsed overhead. He imagined what it might have seen—his months of scavenging, hauling gasoline and explosives through empty streets, his hands trembling as he soaked carpets and stacked propane tanks. He'd thought he was alone, a ghost moving through a graveyard, but the light had been there, a silent witness to his every act. The thought sent a shiver through him, a mix of comfort and unease. He wasn't alone, not entirely, but he didn't know what that meant—not yet.

The night stretched on, the light holding steady, its brightness a constant now rather than a fleeting flare. Bernie sat there, his breath fogging in the brisk air, and let his mind wander.

He pictured the city as it might have been, back when the streets buzzed with life—cars weaving through traffic, voices rising in a chorus of noise, lights flickering in every window. He saw Ellen's face again, or the shadow of it, her smile bright against the hum of a world that moved. Sarah's laughter echoed in his ears, faint and fleeting, a memory he couldn't trust but couldn't let go. Had they been real? Had he lived that life, or had he always been this —alone, watched by a light he didn't understand? The doubt lingered, but it didn't matter as much now. The light was real, and it had seen him. That was enough to keep him going.

He slid off the truck, his boots hitting the ground with a soft thud, and stood beside the gasoline trail, its dark line still waiting for a spark he no longer needed to give. The matchbox sat where he'd left it, a dozen unlit sticks scattered in the dirt, their red tips dull in the light's glow. He bent to pick them up, his fingers carefully gathering the matches and placing them back in the rough wooden container, he tucked it back into his pocket. The city didn't need to burn—not tonight, not like this. The light had answered without fire, and that changed everything. He looked up again, the white brilliance searing into his vision, and felt a spark of something new—curiosity, purpose, a question he'd chase until he understood.

Why had it watched him? Why had it waited? He didn't know, but he would. He'd spent years surviving, repeating the same steps in a world that offered nothing back, but now there was something—a mystery, a connection, a reason to move forward. The light pulsed on, a steady meter, and he nodded to it, a silent promise. He'd find out what it was, what it wanted, why it had chosen him. The silence wasn't absolute anymore; it had a voice, faint and distant, and he'd listen until it spoke.

He turned back toward the house, the light's glow casting his long shadow across the ground, and walked into the night, the question burning brighter than any fire he could have lit.

But why?

7

Weeks had passed since the night sky had been brightened by the light's dazzling display, that sudden eruption of white that had bathed the city in strange, dancing shadows. Bernie was beginning to think he'd imagined it—a fleeting dream born from a mind too long starved of connection. The memory lingered, unanswered and vivid: the match scorching his fingers, the light flaring ten times brighter than the moon, the certainty that he'd been seen. But now, as the days and nights melted together, that certainty frayed, unraveling like the patched threads of his jacket. Every evening, he stepped onto the porch and stared at the sky, his eyes tracing the familiar sprawl of stars. He begged silently, a wordless plea that pulsed in his chest—begged to be seen again, to feel that fleeting thread of something beyond himself. He craved attention, a desperate, gnawing need to know he wasn't alone, that the silence wasn't absolute. The light had given him that once, a taste of meaning, and now its absence of recognition was a curse heavier than he'd ever imagined.

The light was still there, faint as ever, pulsing low against the black—a dim heartbeat he could barely trust. He'd sit on the sagging steps, his ukulele untouched beside him, and watch it, right on schedule, waiting for it to flare again, to acknowledge him as it had before. But it didn't. The stars glittered, cold and indifferent, and the thin crescent moon offered no comfort. The city sprawled beyond the suburb, its buildings dark and still, their gasoline-soaked interiors and explosive caches waiting for a spark he hadn't yet given. He remained alone, the silence pressing in like a weight he couldn't shift, and doubt began to whisper in his ear. Had he imagined everything—the light's response, the shadows dancing, the sense of being watched? Was it another trick, like the voices he'd heard in the wind or the faces he'd seen in the dust? His memory was a fog, a maze of half-truths, and he couldn't be sure—not anymore.

That night—the night it had flared—had cursed him more than he could have foreseen. It had lit a spark of hope, a fragile flame he'd nursed through weeks of watching, only to leave him stranded in its aftermath. He'd thought he'd found a purpose, a connection, but now he was back where he'd started: a man alone, staring at a sky that offered nothing back. The doubt grew, a cold tide rising in his chest, and he couldn't shake it. If the light had reacted to his threat of destruction before, maybe it would again. He'd learned that much—that chaos had provoked it, pulled it out of its silence. With nothing to lose, he put the plan in motion once more, a reckless echo of the months he'd spent scavenging and preparing. The city was still primed, a powder keg of his making, and he'd set it to explode again, a final bid to force the light's attention.

He spent the day checking his work, retracing the steps he'd taken weeks ago. He walked the suburb's edge, his boots crunching on gravel, and inspected the truck—its barren tank still hovering over a dark, shimmering fuse toward the city. He ventured into the streets beyond, the air thick with the faint, sour scent of decay, and tested the gasoline-soaked carpets in the low-rise buildings, their fibers still damp and volatile. The propane tanks stood where he'd left them, strategically placed throughout, their metal surfaces dulled by dust but heavy with potential. The dynamite waited in the taller towers, tucked into corners where it would amplify the blaze. Everything was ready, just as it had been before, a city poised on the edge of ruin. He moved through it all with a quiet determination, his hands steady despite the tremble in his heart, and returned home as the sun dipped low, painting the sky with streaks of orange and gray.

Bernie waited until night, until the dark unfurled its full weight and the stars emerged. He stood beside the truck, the gasoline puddle glinting faintly under the thin moonlight, his walking stick propped against the rusted fender. The matchbox sat heavy in his pocket, a dozen small promises of fire, and he pulled it out, sliding it open with a soft rasp. He'd light a match, just like before, and look to the light, waiting for a reaction—a flare, a pulse, anything to prove he wasn't alone. His breath fogged in the cold air as he scanned the sky, his eyes locking onto the faint glow that appeared right on schedule, its rhythm steady and dim. It hung there, watching him—or so he told himself—and he felt a flicker of the old anticipation, a shadow of the hope he'd once held.

He struck the match.

The flame flared to life with a hiss, a bright tongue dancing at its tip, casting flickering shadows across the ground. He held it, the heat prickling his fingers, and looked to the light, his gaze unwavering. "See me," he whispered, the words lost to the night, a plea he couldn't suppress. He waited, counting the seconds, willing the light to respond as it had before—to erupt in white brilliance, to cast its strange shadows over the city, to prove it cared. But this time, none came. The light pulsed on, faint and unchanged, its beat steady as if he'd done nothing at all. In that moment, hope slipped away, a fragile thread snapping under the weight of silence. A dark doubt surged in its place and he stood there, the match burning, his chest taut with questions. What if he destroyed everything and no one noticed? What if this wasn't what they wanted—what it wanted? The city waited, primed to burn, but the light offered no sign, no answer.

Bernie hesitated, the first match trembling in his hand as the flame crept closer to his skin. It scorched his fingers, a faint sting he barely felt, and went out, a wisp of smoke curling upward into the dark. He stared at the dead stick, his breath shallow, then reached for the matchbox again. He struck another, the flare bright and brief, and lowered it to the gasoline right away, desperation overriding caution. He needed a reaction, needed the fire to force the light's hand. But strangely, just as the flame neared the slick puddle, it went out—a sudden, inexplicable flicker, then nothing. He frowned, his brow furrowing, and struck another, then another, five more in quick succession, each one flaring and dying before it could touch the fuel. The gasoline shimmered below, untouched, as if shielded by an invisible force, a flame-extinguishing wall he couldn't breach.

He dropped to his knees, the matchbox slipping from his hand, its contents scattering across the dirt. His hands shook as he struck one last match, holding it inches from the puddle, willing it to catch. The flame danced, bright and defiant, then sputtered out, leaving him in darkness. No matter what he did, he couldn't destroy—not the city, not the silence, not the emptiness that defined him. The light pulsed on, faint and indifferent, offering no reaction, no recognition. No one noticed his existence, and he was powerless to change it. The realization crashed over him, a wave of despair that drowned the last embers of hope. He'd built a fire to be seen, a scream into the void, but the void had swallowed it whole, leaving him with nothing.

Bernie fell forward, his palms pressing into the cold, damp earth, and wept. The tears came sudden and fierce, a flood he couldn't stop, spilling down his face and soaking into the dirt. His shoulders shook, his breath hitching in ragged sobs, the sound harsh and alien in the stillness. He was truly alone—more alone than he'd ever been, the light's silence a final, crushing proof. It had seen him once, flared in response to his threat, but now it turned away, leaving him to drown in the dark. The city stood intact, its destruction denied, and he knelt there, a man broken by his own futility. The stars glittered above, cold and distant, and the light pulsed on, a faint heartbeat he couldn't reach.

He stayed there, crumpled beside the truck, the gasoline's fumes mingling with the salt of his tears. The heavy night pressed in and he let it take him, his sobs fading into a quiet, shuddering breath. The matchbox lay scattered around him, its sticks useless now, a testament to his failure. He'd begged to be seen, craved it with every fiber of his being, but the light had no answer—not tonight, maybe not ever. The doubt he'd fought so hard to bury surged back, stronger than before, and he wondered if it had all been a lie—his family, his purpose, the light itself. Was he even real, or just a shadow cast by a world that no longer cared?

The light pulsed on, dim and steady, and Bernie wept into the silence, alone.

8

It took many nights of thought, depression, and frustration to reach this point, but in the end, Bernie felt he had no other choice. The silence had won, a relentless tide that drowned every flicker of hope he'd tried to cling to. Since he couldn't destroy all that was around him—the city that refused to burn, the gasoline that mocked his matches with its strange resistance—he would destroy himself. Surely that would get a reaction from the light, a final, undeniable shout in the darkness. And if not, well... he wouldn't have to endure this pitiful existence anymore, this endless loop of loneliness that gnawed at his bones. The thought settled over him, heavy but certain, a dark clarity born from weeks of wrestling with the emptiness. He'd begged to be seen, wept into the dirt when the flames failed, and now he was done—done waiting, done hoping, done with a world that offered nothing back.

It wasn't an easy reality, knowing he was going to kill himself. Bernie stood in the dim light of his house, his hands resting on the cinder-block table, staring at the cracked walls as if they might offer some reprieve. The decision wasn't impulsive; it was a slow, grinding choice, carved out of a past he could barely trust and a present that suffocated him. Once, long ago—or so he believed—he'd been loved. He'd loved in return. He'd had a purpose, a life that thrummed with meaning. He remembered Ellen's warm hands, the way she'd hum softly while cooking, the scent of her hair when she leaned close. He saw Sarah's small face, her eyes bright with wonder, her laughter a melody that once filled the very house he stood in. He'd loved life more than most, waking each day with a quiet joy, a mechanic's steady hands fixing what was broken, a father and husband who built something worth keeping. Now he had nothing—no family, no sound, no echo of that love. Whether it was real or a trick of his fractured memory, it didn't matter. It was gone, and he was left with the husk of a man he didn't recognize.

Either way it went, he would no longer feel lonely. In Bernie's mind, there were two possible outcomes, stark and simple, like the lines he'd once scratched on paper to track the light. He'd try to off himself and get a reaction—a flare, a pulse, something to confirm he wasn't alone. Maybe, just maybe, it would give him direction, a purpose to live, a reason to pull himself out of the dark. Or he'd succeed, and the struggles of this new, desolate world would fade— no more scavenging roots in the cold, no more nights staring at a sky that didn't care, no more being alone. He turned the possibilities over in his mind, weighing them like stones, and found a strange peace in their finality. One way or another, the silence would end.

He knew how he'd do it—short, simple, and to the point. Long ago, he'd raided a local gun store, back when he'd thought he might need to defend his position, his patch of earth in a world gone quiet. He'd hauled a shotgun from the shattered display case, its barrel cold and heavy in his hands, and kept it stashed in a corner of the house, wrapped in an old blanket. He'd since learned there was nothing and no one to defend against— no threats, no shadows, just the endless nothing. Still, he had it, a tool he'd never fired but always known was there. It waited for him now, a silent promise of release, and he felt its pull as he moved through the day, his last day, with a quiet resolve.

Bernie spent that day doing things he used to love, rituals from a life he could barely grasp but wanted to honor, just in case the light didn't care. He woke early, the sky a pale gray beyond the boarded-up window, and made a delicious breakfast—his version of it, anyway, in this barren world. He dug wild onions from the patch near the river, their fragrant scent cutting through the damp air, and mashed them into a paste with a flat stone. He mixed them with a handful of dried berries from the burlap sack, softening them over the fire in his dented pot until they formed a tart, warm mash. He ate slowly, standing on the porch, the taste bittersweet on his tongue, a faint echo of meals shared with others —or so he imagined. It held little meaning now, but he forced himself to savor it, to feel the texture against his teeth, to pretend it mattered.

After breakfast, he hiked through the suburb, his walking stick tapping against the ground, the grass flowing in the breeze. He climbed a low hill he'd once loved, its slope gentle but enough to make his breath ragged, and stood at the top, looking out over the city's jagged skyline. The buildings on the brink of collapse, their windows dark, their walls crumbling under the weight of time. He lingered there, the wind tugging at his jacket, and tried to find beauty in the stillness, in the way the light slanted across the ruins. It was a hollow effort, but he stayed until the ache in his legs forced him back down. At home, he picked up the ukulele, its chipped wood rough against his palms, and strummed a few chords—soft, aimless notes that drifted into the emptiness. The sound was thin, swallowed by the silence, but he played anyway, his fingers remembering a tune he couldn't place, a melody from a life that might have been.

Later, he took a long walk, wandering past the houses that lined his street, their lawns overgrown with thistles and dandelions. He followed the riverbank, its waters still flat and lifeless, reflecting the sky in a dull sheen. The scenery was beautiful in its way—the reeds bending in the wind, the earth rich with the scent of damp soil—but it felt distant, a painting he couldn't step into. He walked until his legs burned, until the sun dipped low, and returned home with a heaviness he couldn't shake. These things—cooking, hiking, music, the walk—were shadows of joy, rituals he performed for a man he used to be. He'd tried to enjoy them, to wring some meaning from his last day, but they slipped through his fingers like sand.

At dusk, he made his favorite dinner of this desolate world—a stew of roots and berries, seasoned with wild herbs he'd found near the old garden a few streets over. He cooked it slow over the fire, the flames crackling in the hearth, and carried it outside to the porch. He sat on the steps, the bowl warm in his hands, and ate while viewing a spectacular sunset—the most vivid he'd ever seen. The sky blazed with orange and purple, streaks of color bleeding together in a fierce, fleeting display that lit the world below. He chewed slowly, the flavors faint but comforting, and watched the sun sink, its glow fading into a deep, endless black. It was beautiful, a final gift he hadn't expected, and he let it linger in his chest as night fell.

When the dark settled in, he spied the faint glimmer of the elusive light in the sky, pulsing low and steady, right on schedule. Bernie stood, his breath shallow, and moved with purpose. He dragged a chair from the house—an old wooden thing, its legs wobbling but sturdy enough—and placed it outside, in the open yard near the house, in full view of the light. He sat down, the seat a firm foundation under his weight, and straightened his pants and shirt, smoothing the fabric with hands that trembled faintly. He reached for the shotgun, propped against the wall where he'd left it, and pulled it into his lap. The metal was cold, its weight a solid anchor against his thighs, he racked the gun and rested the end of the barrel under his chin, the muzzle pressing into the soft flesh there. His breath steadied, the air a gentle reminder of this world against his face, and he adjusted his grip, the stock firm against the chair.

He put his thumb on the trigger, the metal smooth and firm, and looked directly at the faint light, its glow a dim heartbeat against the stars. He stared, hoping beyond all hope that it would show some flicker of recognition—a flare, a pulse, anything to stop him. He searched its rhythm for meaning, for a sign that it cared, but deep down, he knew it wouldn't. The light, like all other things—himself included—really didn't care. It had flared once, long ago, but now it watched in silence, a distant witness to a man it wouldn't save. His chest tightened, a mix of resignation and despair, and he felt the tears prick at his eyes, hot and unwanted. He'd wanted to be seen, to matter, but the silence was absolute, and he was done fighting it.

Bernie pulled the trigger.

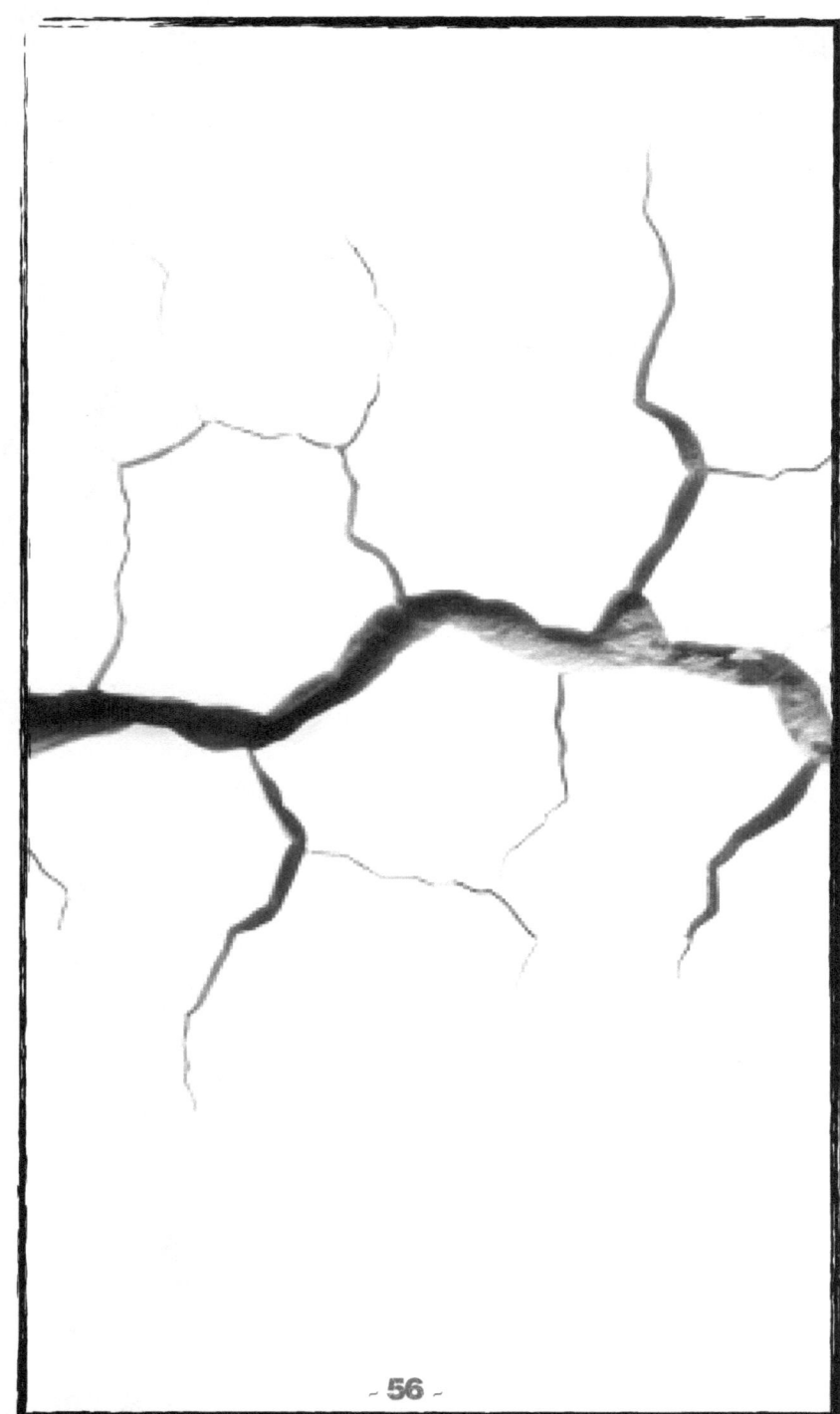

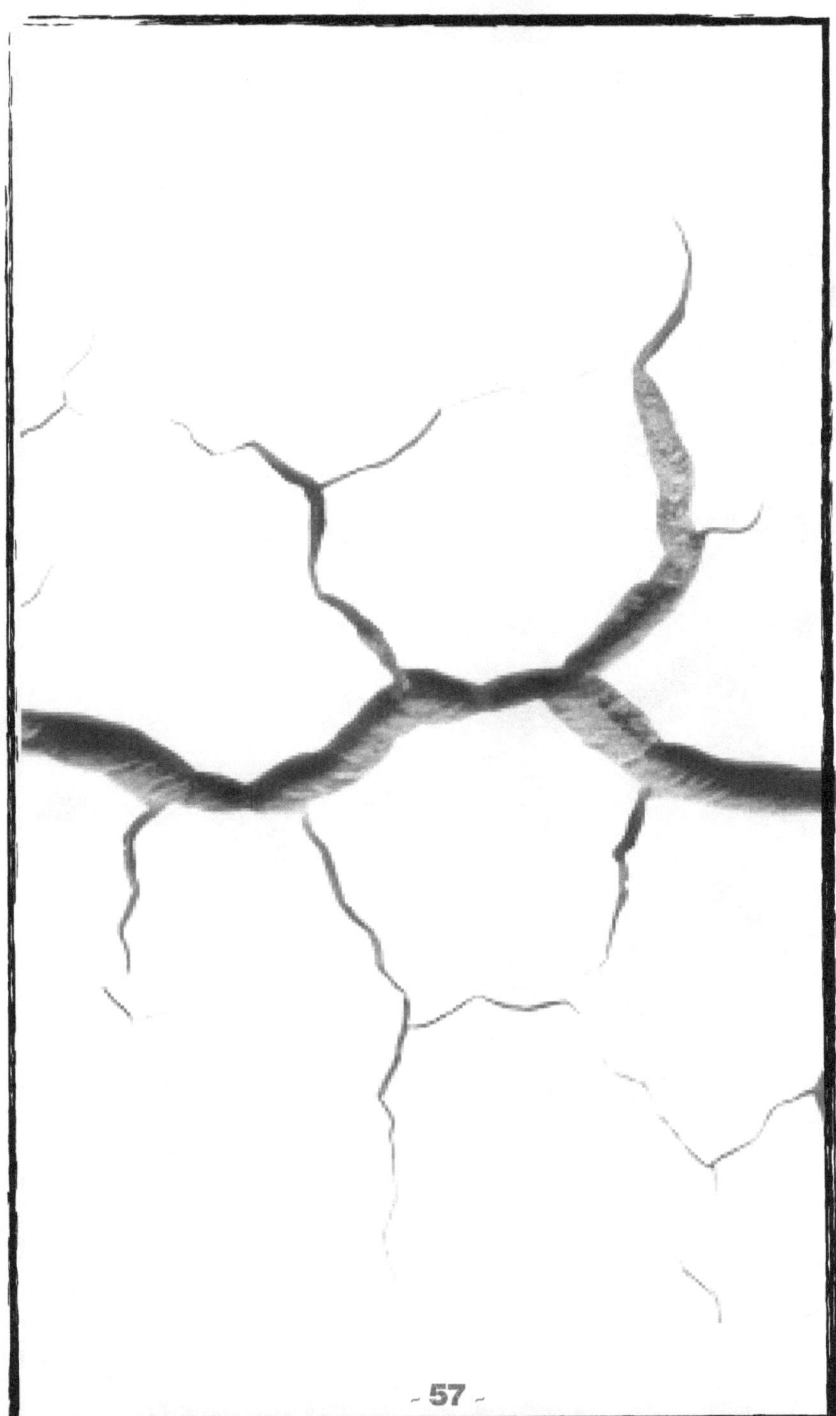

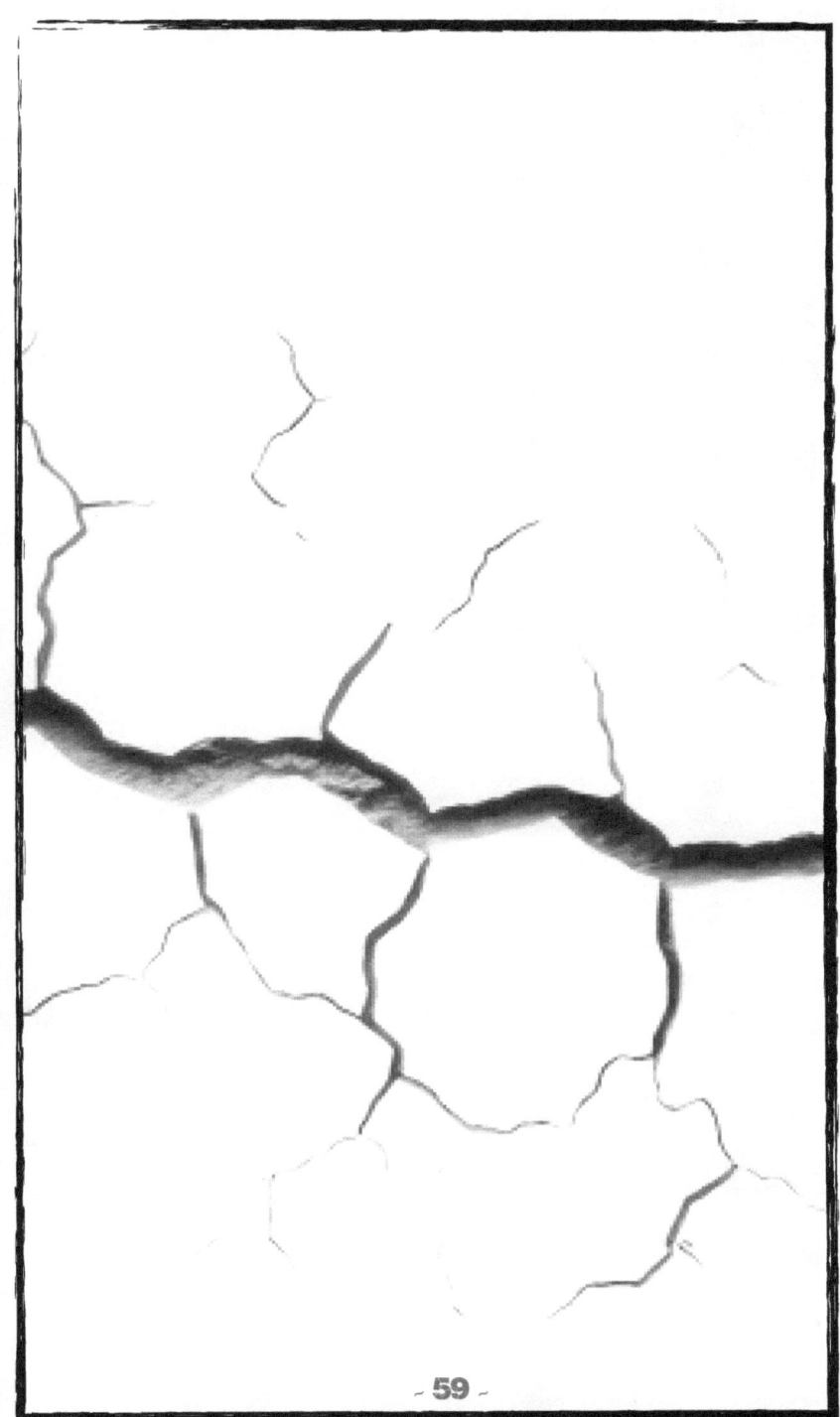

Click

Bernie opened his eyes, the dull sound echoing in his ears, sharp and hollow against the night's stillness. His breath caught, a silent plea in the cool air, and he blinked, disoriented, his hands trembling around the shotgun's grip. Had he forgotten to load the gun? No—he'd checked multiple times, his fingers tracing the shells in the chamber with a meticulous care born of resolve. He could still feel the weight of them, the cold metal smooth against his skin as he'd slid them in, one by one, before dragging the chair outside. The barrel rested under his chin, its muzzle pressing into the soft flesh, and his finger hovered over the trigger, frozen in the aftermath of that empty sound. His heart thudded, a frantic rhythm against his ribs, and he looked up at the light once more, its faint pulse steady against the black sky. Tears welled in his eyes, hot and stinging, obscuring the glow into a hazy smear. No reaction—no flare, no shift, just the same dim heartbeat he'd begged to notice him.

A feeling of desperation gnawed at his insides, a wild, gnashing thing that tore at the fragile threads of his composure.

Maybe the gun had malfunctioned, some rusted mechanism failing him at the last moment. He lowered the shotgun, his hands shaking as he fumbled with the chamber, the metal cold and unyielding under his fingers. He pried it open, the hinges squeaking faintly, and peered inside. The shells were there, glinting dully in the starlight—definitely loaded, just as he'd left them. His brow furrowed, confusion warring with the despair that churned in his gut, and he snapped the chamber shut, the click a small, defiant sound in the silence. He lifted the barrel again, pressing it hard against his chin, the edge biting into his skin, and took one deep breath, the air cutting and cold in his lungs. He steadied himself, his eyes locked on the light, and pulled the trigger.

Click

He squeezed his eyes shut, a low groan escaping his throat as the sound mocked him once more. The barrel stayed against his chin, its weight a cruel anchor, and he pressed it harder, as if force alone could make it work. His finger tightened on the trigger again—*click*—and again—*click*—and again—*click*—each empty snap a hammer blow to his fraying resolve. Nothing happened, no blast, no end, just the relentless silence stretching out around him. His breath came in short, ragged bursts, his chest heaving as frustration surged, hot and bitter, drowning the despair in a flood of rage. He yanked the shotgun away, his arms trembling with the effort, and threw it as far as he could, a primal yell tearing from his throat as it arced through the night.

BANG!

The sound was deafening, a thunderous roar that split the air and shook the ground beneath him. Bernie stumbled back, his ears ringing, his eyes wide with shock as the shotgun landed a dozen yards away, its tip smoking from the freshly expelled shell. A plume of dirt rose where it hit, the grass singed black around it, and the acrid scent of gunpowder drifted toward him, smoky and biting. He stood there, frozen, his breath stopped as he stared at the smoldering barrel, the echo of the blast reverberating in his skull. It was louder than he could have ever imagined, a sound that shattered the silence he'd lived in for years, a violent proof that the gun worked—just not for him. His hands clenched into fists, his nails digging into his palms, and he took a shaky step forward, then another, drawn to the weapon like a moth to a flame.

He picked up the still-smoldering shotgun, its metal warm against his skin, the barrel radiating heat from the shot it had finally fired. His fingers brushed the ejected shell, its casing glinting faintly in the dirt, and he bent to retrieve it, rolling it between his thumb and forefinger. It was spent, empty, but the chamber held more—he knew it did. But just to make sure, he reached into his pocket, pulling a fresh shell from the small stash he'd carried out, and loaded it with a practiced motion, the click of it sliding into place a small, hollow comfort. He racked and lifted the gun again, pressing the barrel back under his chin, the muzzle hot now, a faint burn against his flesh. He stared at the light, its pulse unchanged, and felt a sob catch in his throat, a desperate plea he couldn't voice. One last time—he'd try one last time. His thumb found the trigger, his hand steady despite the tears streaming down his face, and he pulled.

Click

The sound was a knife, cutting through the last of his hope, and Bernie fell to the ground, the shotgun slipping from his grasp. He hit the dirt hard, his knees buckling under him, and wept, the tears coming in a flood he couldn't stop. His shoulders shook, his breath hitching in ragged, broken sobs that tore from his chest, loud and raw in the stillness. The light pulsed on, faint and indifferent, a silent witness to his collapse, and he pressed his palms into the earth, the cold soil gritty against his skin. He cried for the life he'd lost—or thought he'd lost—for the love he couldn't prove, for the purpose that had slipped away. He cried for the city that wouldn't burn, the matches that failed, the gun that refused him. He cried until his throat burned, until his eyes ached, until the emotional toll of the day—the weight of his last breakfast, his hike, his music, his sunset—crushed him into the ground.

He didn't know how long he wept, time muddled into a haze of grief and exhaustion. The night pressed in and the stars glittering above like cold, distant eyes. The light pulsed on, its rhythm a cruel metronome to his despair, and he felt it watching, its silence a final judgment. His sobs slowed, fading into shuddering breaths, and his body grew heavy, the strength leaching from his limbs. He slumped forward, his forehead resting against the dirt, the shotgun lying beside him, its barrel dark and still. The world spun, a dizzying tilt of stars and shadows, and he passed out, the emotional toll dragging him under like a tide he couldn't fight. Bernie did not wish to wake— not to this, not to the silence, not to a life that refused to let him go.

The night stretched on, the air settling over him like a shroud. The chair stood empty behind him, its wood shaking faintly in the breeze, a mute sentinel to his fall. The shotgun gleamed in the starlight, its metal cooling now, the fresh shell still loaded, waiting for a purpose it wouldn't fulfill. The gasoline fuse shimmered nearby, untouched, a dark trail leading nowhere. Bernie lay there, sprawled in the dirt, his breath shallow and uneven, his face streaked with tears and grime. The light pulsed above, faint and steady, offering no answers, no comfort, no change. It hung there, a dim heartbeat in a sky that didn't care, and the silence held him, as it always had—unbroken, unyielding, absolute.

He'd tried to destroy himself, to force a reaction or an end, but even that had been denied him. The gun worked—he'd seen it, heard it—but not when it touched him, not when he needed it to. It was as if the world itself refused his exit, trapping him in a limbo he couldn't escape. The desperation that had mauled him earlier softened into a dull, aching void, a resignation that seeped into his bones as he lay unconscious. He'd wanted to be seen, to matter, to break the silence with a final act, but the light had turned away, and the shotgun had betrayed him. He was alone—truly, irrevocably alone—and the realization followed him into the dark, a shadow he couldn't outrun.

The stars wheeled overhead, the night deepening, and Bernie slept, his body curled against the earth, his mind lost to a blackness he hoped would last. The light pulsed on, its glow faint but persistent, a mystery he couldn't solve, a presence he couldn't reach. The suburb lay quiet around him, its houses sagging under the weight of time, their windows dark and empty. The river flowed in the distance and the wind whispered through the grass, a sound too soft to wake him. He'd given everything—his hope, his rage, his tears—and it hadn't been enough. The silence held him, a prison he couldn't burn or break, and he surrendered to it, lost in a sleep he didn't want to end.

PART 2

10

He appeared in a field, lying flat on his back, the sensation of soft earth pressing against him unfamiliar after so long on rusty springs, hard floors, or cracked concrete. Bernie opened his eyes, blinking against a sudden, dazzling brightness that stung after the dim haze of his last memory. The first thing he saw was the brightest blue sky, a vast, endless expanse that stretched above him, unmarred by the gray smudges of smoke or the weight of silence he'd grown accustomed to. He turned his head, his cheek brushing against blades of grass—vivid green, lush and alive, stretching as far as the eye could see in every direction. A light breeze danced across the field, whispering through the stalks, and it grazed his skin, cool and gentle, carrying a faint scent of earth and something sweet he couldn't place. A couple of clouds lingered in the sky, soft and white, drifting lazily like cotton caught on a current. It was a picture-perfect day, a scene so pristine it felt unreal, as if he'd stumbled into a painting from a life he'd forgotten.

Waking in an unfamiliar place, most would feel afraid—heart racing, senses sharp with the instinct to flee or fight. Bernie felt oddly calm, a quiet stillness settling over him like a blanket. It was a drastic change from how he'd felt when he'd finally fallen asleep, crumpled in the dirt beside the truck, his tears soaking into the earth after the night's failed attempts at suicide. The shotgun's hollow clicks still echoed in his mind, each one a taunt, a refusal to let him go. He'd passed out then, exhausted and broken, wishing for an end—any end—to the loneliness that had consumed him. Now, here he was, sprawled in a field under a sky too beautiful to belong to the world he'd known, and the despair that had once enveloped him felt distant, muted, as if it belonged to someone else.

Bernie sat up slowly, his hands pressing into the grass, its texture soft and yielding under his palms. He stood, his boots sinking slightly into the soil, and turned in a slow circle, looking around for any sign of life other than himself—any hint of civilization, a building, a road, a shadow that wasn't his own. Nothing. Nothing but the picture-perfect scenery unfurling endlessly around him—green hills rolling gently into the distance, the sky a seamless blue, the breeze stirring the grass in waves that shimmered like water under the sun. He desperately needed interaction, a voice to break the silence, a presence to prove he wasn't alone, but as he scanned the horizon, he found only emptiness. He exhaled, a faint laugh escaping his lips, dry and brittle. "Well... could be worse," he thought to himself, the words forming silently in his mind. It was definitely an upgrade from the deserted, post-apocalyptic landscape he'd somehow been transported from—the crumbling houses, the ash-choked streets, the river that reflected nothing but a dead sky. This was beauty, pure and untouched, and yet it left him hollow, a man adrift in a paradise he didn't understand.

He didn't know how he'd arrived here, in this place of vivid green and endless light. The last thing he remembered was the dirt against his face, the shotgun's barrel cooling beside him, the faint pulse of the light in the sky as he slipped into unconsciousness. He'd grown to believe he didn't deserve such beauty—years of isolation, of scavenging roots and berries in a world that offered no kindness, had convinced him he was a relic, a ghost unworthy of anything but decay. Yet here he was, standing in a field that seemed to mock that belief with its vibrancy. Had he died after all, slipped past the shotgun's refusal into some afterlife? Or had the light—the light that had watched him, flared once, then ignored him—done this, plucked him from his ruin and dropped him here? The questions churned in his mind, but they didn't sharpen into fear. He felt calm, detached, as if the answers didn't matter as much as the fact that he was standing, breathing, alive.

Bernie began walking. He picked a direction—east, he guessed, judging by the sun's position—and moved forward, his boots brushing through the grass with a soft rustle. The breeze followed him, light against his cheek, tugging at his patched jacket as he went. He traveled for hours, the landscape stretching out unchanging, a seamless expanse of green and blue that offered no landmarks, no variation. The sun climbed higher, its warmth soaking into his shoulders, but he felt no hunger, no gnawing ache in his stomach that had once driven him to forage. His legs didn't tire, his breath didn't shorten; he just walked, step after step, the rhythm steady and unbroken. It was strange, unnatural, this lack of fatigue, but he didn't question it. The field rolled on, endless and perfect, and he let it carry him forward, a man moving through a dream he couldn't wake from.

The sun began to set, painting the sky with streaks of gold and pink, a slow descent that softened the blue into twilight. Bernie wasn't the least bit tired, his body untouched by the exhaustion he'd known in the old world, but out of habit, he decided it was time to rest. The day had been long, not in effort but in hours, and the ritual of stopping felt right, a tether to the man he'd been. Finding a place wasn't hard—everywhere was exactly the same, a uniform stretch of grass and sky with no trees, no rocks, no shelter to distinguish one spot from another. He sat down, the earth cozy beneath him, and leaned back on his hands, the blades tickling his palms. Twilight came, a gentle fade from gold to purple, and then night fell, the sky deepening into a rich, velvety black.

Bernie stared upward, expecting the familiar sprawl of stars, the glittering map he'd traced for years. He was surprised—shocked, even—by the total lack of them. The sky was empty, a void unbroken by twinkles, its vastness stark and absolute. The moon shone bright, a full, silver disc that cast a pale glow over the field, its light pooling in the grass like spilled milk. But the stars were gone, erased from a sky he'd always known, and the absence left him unsettled, a quiet ache in his chest. He lay back, the earth cradling him, and searched the darkness, his breath steady but his mind turning. Where was he? What was this place, so beautiful by day yet so hollow by night?

Then... he saw it. The same familiar light in the sky that had shown itself to him in the city, pulsing faintly as it always had. But this time, it wasn't high above, a distant speck he couldn't reach. It appeared on the horizon, close to the land, its glow low and steady, a beacon cutting through the empty black. He sat up, his heart thudding, and squinted at it, the pulse clearer now, more defined. It was far—miles, maybe days away—but Bernie knew it was closer than it had ever been, tethered to the earth in a way that felt tangible, real. The light had followed him here—or brought him here—and its presence stirred something in him, a flicker of the old curiosity, the old need to understand. He must continue walking. The journey would be long, the field stretching endlessly before him, but the reward could be great— answers, connection, a purpose he'd lost.

He stood, brushing the grass from his hands, and faced the light, its glow a faint heartbeat against the horizon. The moon lit his path, casting his shadow long and swaying across the field, and he took a step, then another, the breeze whispering at his back. He didn't know what lay ahead—whether the light would flare again, whether it would lead him to something or nothing— but he had to find out. The calm that had settled over him held, a quiet resolve that steadied his steps, and he walked into the night, the endless green fading into shadow around him. The sky remained starless, the moon a solitary guide, and the light pulsed on, calling him forward.

Bernie moved through the dark, his boots rustling the grass, the air cool against his face. He felt no hunger, no fatigue, only the pull of the light, a thread of hope or fate he couldn't ignore. The field stretched on, unchanging, a perfect prison or a perfect promise—he couldn't tell which. But he walked, hour after hour, the horizon very slowly creeping closer with every step, the light growing ever so slightly more distinct. The journey was long, a test of will in a world that defied time, but he pressed on, driven by the memory of the city, the shotgun, the silence he'd escaped. The reward, if it came, could be everything—a voice, a presence, a reason to be. He didn't look back, didn't question how he'd arrived here. He just walked, the light his compass, the field his path, and the night his witness.

11

The moon did little to light the landscape, its silver glow a faint shimmer that barely pierced the endless field stretching out before Bernie. The grass swayed under its weak illumination, a sea of shadow and green that melted into a formless void beyond the reach of his eyes. All of his focus was locked on the bright light lingering on the horizon, a pulsing beacon that sliced through the dark like a blade through cloth. It was his guide, his only anchor in this starless night, and each step toward it felt precarious, a blind plunge into nothingness where the ground might vanish beneath him without warning. He moved forward, his boots brushing through the grass with a soft rustle, the sound swallowed by the vast emptiness that pressed in from all sides. The breeze whispered at his back, refreshing and insistent, tugging at his patched jacket, but it carried no comfort—only a reminder of the abyss he walked through, a blackness that seemed to breathe around him.

Bernie continued walking, his eyes fixed on the light, its glow a distant promise that tethered him to something—anything —in this surreal, endless place. As the moon floated through the sky, arcing slowly overhead, he noticed the light on the horizon growing larger—not brighter yet, but wider, its edges dilating with each step, a subtle sign that he was headed in the right direction. It was a reassurance, faint but real, a whisper that his trek wasn't aimless, that he wasn't circling back into the nothingness he'd woken to. His breath rose in the night air, a steady rhythm that matched his stride, and he clung to that small victory, the light's growth a thread of purpose in a world without form. But beneath that resolve, a knot of fear tightened in his chest. What if he didn't reach it by morning? If the sun rose, its glare would swallow the glow, leaving him lost again in this boundless land of green and blue, a daylight sea with no shores, no markers. He'd be adrift, directionless, and the thought chilled him—it was in the dark that light shone clearest, and he needed this night to hold, to guide him to whatever waited ahead.

He willed the night to stay, a desperate, silent plea that pulsed with every beat of his heart. The moon hung above, its pale disc a solitary sentinel, and he glanced at it now and then, as if his stare could anchor it in place, could stretch the hours before dawn swallowed his path. He pressed on, the field rolling out unchanging, its grass a uniform carpet that vanished into the black beyond his sight. It felt like hours—hours of the same soft rustle underfoot, hours of the breeze grazing his cheek, hours of staring at that distant glow—but fatigue and hunger still didn't touch him. His legs carried him without protest, his stomach stayed silent, no ache or growl to mark the time. Something about this place kept normal human needs at bay, a strange suspension that left him weightless, untethered from the body he'd known in the city. It was unsettling, this absence of weariness, but he didn't linger on it. The light was his focus, his sole reason, and he followed it, step after step, into the void that stretched around him.

The light on the horizon continued to grow slowly with each stride, its pulse more distinct, a heartbeat he could almost feel thrumming in his chest. It was closer—he was certain now—though the distance remained a mystery, the field's endless expanse warping his sense of near and far. He squinted at it, the glow a soft smear against the black, and felt determination harden within him, a quiet fire that had flickered out in the city but now burned anew. He was making progress, inching toward the answer he'd chased since the shotgun's hollow clicks, since the light had flared and then turned away. He'd continue, he decided—even if it took years, even if this journey stretched into an eternity of steps through this unchanging green. Time didn't matter here, not in a place where hunger and fatigue were ghosts, where the night could linger forever if he asked it to. He'd walk until he reached the light, until he understood why it had brought him here, until it gave him something to hold—a purpose, a presence, a break in the silence.

The moon lingered overhead, its arc halted at its peak, a silver eye frozen in the sky. Bernie noticed it as he walked, his gaze flicking upward, a faint crease etching his brow. It hadn't shifted—not in hours, not since he'd set out toward the light. The realization settled over him, quiet and strange, another thread in the tapestry of this place that defied the world he'd known. The night wasn't just long; it was still, as if time itself had paused, holding its breath to watch him chase the glow on the horizon. He didn't know if it was mercy or a cage, but it kept his direction clear, the light steady against the dark, and he clung to that clarity, his boots pressing into the grass with a resolve he hadn't felt since the dream of a city in ashes. The breeze carried no scent now, just a cool, clean touch that brushed his face and stirred the stalks in gentle waves, and he let it guide him, a silent companion in a world that offered no other.

He walked on, the field vast and never-ending, its beauty laced with a quiet menace he couldn't shake. The light grew larger, its edges still sharpening, a pulse that seemed to call him closer, and he let it pull him forward, his steps steady, his breath even. The moon's faint glow painted the grass in silver streaks, but it was the light on the horizon that lit his way, a beacon he couldn't turn from. He didn't know how long he'd been walking—hours, days, the night blurring into itself—but he didn't falter, didn't slow. The field stretched on, endless and perfect, and he moved through it, a lone figure in a landscape that held no answers, only the promise of the light. He felt the weight of it now, the pull of something he couldn't name, and he leaned into it, his heart thudding with a mix of hope and dread. The silence was absolute, the breeze too soft to break it, and he walked deeper into the dark, the glow his only star in a sky that had none.

Then, out of the black abyss that surrounded him, Bernie heard a low moan.

The sound sliced through the silence, deep and resonant, a vibration that rolled across the field and into his bones. The hairs on his neck stood on end, a prickling wave that raced down his spine and rooted him to the spot, his boot frozen mid-step above the grass. His breath caught, a gasp that hung in the air, and his heart slammed against his ribs, a frantic drumbeat that drowned out the breeze. The moan lingered, a low, mournful note that seemed to rise from the earth itself, from the shadows that pooled around him, from the endless dark he'd walked into. It wasn't the wind—he knew its sigh, its gentle rustle—and it wasn't his mind, not this time. He'd heard ghosts in the city, whispers that faded when he turned, but this was real, a presence that gripped him with icy fingers and held him fast. Terror—pure, paralyzing terror—flooded him, a cold tide that locked his limbs and widened his eyes, his gaze darting into the blackness that swallowed the field.

12

Bernie stood completely still, fear paralyzing his body like a cold, iron vise clamped around his limbs. His breath hitched in his throat, shallow and ragged, a vast contrast to the still night air, but he couldn't move, couldn't speak. He tried to ask, "Who's there?"—a desperate reflex from a time when questions had answers—but no sound escaped his lips, his voice trapped behind a wall of terror that choked him silent. The low moan had pierced the silence, a sound so alien, so *wrong* in this endless field, that it rooted him to the spot, his boots glued to the earth as if the grass itself held him captive. It had been so long since he'd heard anything beyond the wind's whisper or the slow crumble of the buildings he'd once called home—years, maybe decades, of nothing but decay and his own footsteps. Yet he knew he'd heard something, a deep, resonant groan that wasn't a trick of his fractured mind. It was real, and it terrified him in a way the city's silence never had.

His mind sharpened, narrowing to a single, razor-edged focus: where had the noise come from? Bernie's ears perked, straining against the stillness, ready to catch the faintest hint of sound, to pinpoint its source in the black abyss that swallowed the field. He tilted his head slightly, his neck stiff with tension, his pulse thudding in his temples like heavy steps he couldn't quiet. A breeze brushed his cheek, a soft rustle through the grass, but it was too familiar, too gentle to be the culprit. He waited, his breath held tight, his body a statue in the dark, every nerve alight with the anticipation of that moan returning. Silence reigned, heavy and absolute—not even the crunch of movement on the black grass, not a whisper of anything beyond his own ragged breathing. The field stretched out around him, broad and unseen, a void that seemed to mock his stillness with its indifference.

He damned himself for willing the dark to stay, a bitter curse that echoed in his skull. Hours ago—or days, time didn't matter here—he'd begged the night to linger, to keep the light on the horizon clear, to guide him through this endless green. Now that darkness was a prison, a shroud that hid whatever had made that horrible sound, leaving him blind and vulnerable under the moon's feeble glow. If only he had more light, something stronger than the silver disc overhead or the... Bernie's thoughts stumbled, a jolt of memory cutting through the fog of fear. The light—the pulsing glow on the horizon, the beacon he'd chased since waking in this field. He'd forgotten it in the panic, his mind consumed by the moan, but it was his purpose, his direction. He turned toward it, his boots scuffing the grass, his eyes searching the black where it had hung, steady and growing with every step.

The light was gone.

His heart lurched, a cold spike of dread piercing his chest, and he spun in a slow circle, his gaze sweeping the horizon. Maybe he'd lost it somehow, misplaced it among the chaos of his thoughts, the terror that scrambled his senses. He turned fully, his breath shallow and quick, scanning every inch of the pitch-black landscape for that familiar pulse. Nothing. The only light that peeked through this endless dark was the moon, its pale glow a weak, solitary pinprick against the void. The stars were still absent, the sky a blank slate, and the light—the one thing he'd clung to, the one thing that had given him direction—was nowhere to be seen. He stopped, facing the direction he'd been walking, and stared into the blackness, his hands clenching into fists at his sides. Had it abandoned him, too? Had it flickered out, or had it never been real—a mirage, like the voices he'd heard in the city, like the life he couldn't prove?

Grooooooan

Bernie froze again, the sound slithering through the dark, deeper and more guttural than before. It rolled across the field like a wave, a low, spine-chilling note that vibrated in his chest and set his teeth on edge. He wasn't prepared—not for this, not for the way it sank into his bones, heavy and ominous, a presence he couldn't see. His head snapped to the right, then the left, his eyes wide and darting, searching the shadows that pooled around him. Nothing but black—black grass, black sky, black everything, an abyss that swallowed sight and sound alike. The moan faded, leaving a ringing silence in its wake, but it lingered in his mind, a haunting echo that coiled around his thoughts and squeezed. His breath came faster now and he felt the field shrink around him, the vastness tightening into a cage of unseen threats.

Now, scared and alone, Bernie had nothing—no light, no direction, no hope to cling to. The calm he'd felt waking in this field, the quiet resolve that had carried him through so much walking, shattered under the weight of that second groan. He was completely torn apart, his mind a storm of fear and confusion, his body trembling as the reality of his isolation crashed over him. He dropped to the ground, his knees buckling under him, and hit the grass hard, the soft earth yielding beneath his weight. He shook uncontrollably, his hands gripping the stalks, his shoulders hunching as the terror took hold. Bernie had never known this much fear—not in the city, not with the shotgun under his chin, not even when the matches failed and the silence mocked him. This was different, primal, a dread that crawled through his insides and left him wheezing, a man stripped bare in a darkness that breathed.

As he lay there, shaking and alone, he willed whatever was out there to show itself. His thoughts screamed it, a desperate plea he couldn't voice—*come out, face me, let me see you.* At least then he'd know what he was up against, whether it was the light playing tricks, a shadow given voice, or something worse lurking in this endless field. The uncertainty was a knife, twisting deeper with every shuddering breath, and he'd rather face a monster than cower in the dark, blind and helpless. He pressed his palms into the grass, the blades encircling his skin, and waited, his ears straining for the next sound, his body tensed against the fear that pinned him down.

Hours passed—or what felt like hours, time a meaningless nothing in this night that refused to end. Every so often, the low, spine-chilling groan would drift through the dark, faint and distant, a reminder that he wasn't alone but might as well be. It came from different directions each time—or so he thought, the sound bouncing through the void, impossible to pin down. He tried to track it, his head jerking toward each new echo, but the blackness offered no clues, no shapes, no hints of movement. No way to know which direction to travel, Bernie stayed still, curled on the ground, his hands pressed into the earth, his breath shallow and uneven. The moon hung overhead, its glow a cruel tease that lit nothing beyond the grass at his feet, and he felt the weight of his solitude press harder, a burden he couldn't shake.

Two things happened almost simultaneously, a sudden shift that snapped him out of his trembling stupor. The moon set, its silver light winking out as it slipped below the horizon, plunging everything into complete darkness. The field vanished, the grass swallowed by a black so absolute it felt solid, a wall he couldn't see through. Bernie lifted his hands inches from his face, his fingers trembling, and saw nothing—not even the outline, not a shadow of movement. The world was gone, erased in an instant, and a quick inhale proved the air was suddenly ice cold in his lungs. And then, in that same breath, he felt a slight tickle on his shoulder—a faint, feather-light touch that sent a jolt through him. He stopped shaking, his body locking up, every nerve alight with the sensation. Slowly, the tickle grew, increasing in pressure, and suddenly a full grip encircled his upper arm, a hand's firm grasp, its fingers digging into his flesh through the fabric of his jacket.

A flash of light burst in Bernie's mind—not in the sky, not in the field, but behind his eyes, a blinding white that seared through the dark. He reacted instantly, terror fueling his strength, and twisted away from the haunting grasp, wrenching his arm free with a desperate yank. The grip slipped, the pressure vanishing as quickly as it had come, and he stumbled to his feet, his boots digging into the earth. His heart struggling to keep up with his mind, a frantic beat that drowned out the silence, and he ran—ran into the dark, blind and wild, his arms outstretched to catch whatever lay ahead. He was much too afraid to look back, too afraid to see what had touched him, what had groaned, what waited in the blackness he'd left behind. The field swallowed his footsteps, the grass rustling in his wake, and he fled, a man chased by shadows he couldn't face, into a night that offered no end.

13

Bernie ran and ran, his boots pounding the grass, the sound swallowed by the pitch-black void that enveloped him. He didn't know how far he'd gone—yards, miles, a meaningless measure in a world where distance and darkness were parallel. In this strange place, he never felt exhausted, his legs pumping without ache, his breath steady despite the panic that clawed at his chest. The land stayed dark, an unbroken night that offered no hint of dawn, no shift in the shadows to mark the passage of time. He couldn't tell how long he'd been running, the field stretching endlessly around him, a silent expanse that defied the rules of the world he'd known. All he knew, all that drove him, was that *something* had grabbed him, its grip a cold, constant pressure on his arm, a sensation so foreign it burned into his memory like a brand.

It had been so long since he'd felt any contact with another being—years of solitude in the city, his hands brushing only dust and decay, his skin untouched by anything but the wind. The fact that in this dark world lurked something that could find him, could reach out and hold him, was terrifying—a violation of the silence he'd come to accept as absolute. His mind raced as his feet did, replaying the moment: the tickle on his shoulder, the slow tightening into a full grasp, the flash of light in his head that had freed him. What was it? A hand, yes, but whose? The questions spun, spiraling and relentless, fueling his flight into the black. The field offered no answers, its grass rustling under his boots, the air fresh and heavy against his face, and he ran, blind and wild, driven by a fear so deep it drowned out reason.

Eventually, his pace slowed, not from fatigue—there was none—but from a creeping realization that seeped through the panic. He hadn't tripped, hadn't stumbled, not once in all that running. He couldn't see more than a foot in front of him, the darkness so thick it felt solid, yet his steps had landed steady, the ground unbroken by roots or dips or anything to snag his boots. He eased to a jog, then a walk, his breath slowing, his heart still thudding but no longer deafening. It was strange—impossible, even—this flawless stride through a landscape he couldn't see. In the city, he'd tripped over rubble, caught his feet on cracked pavement, but here, the field was a perfect plane, a smooth expanse that held him up even as it hid itself from his eyes. He stopped, his body straining in the stillness, and stood there, the silence pressing in, the breeze a faint whisper against his cheek. How long had he run? Minutes? Days? He'd never know, time a ghost in this place where a hoped for night reigned eternal.

Standing in the pitch dark, with no direction and no purpose, Bernie felt the weight of his isolation settle over him like a shroud. The terror still lingered, a cold thread woven into his thoughts, but given the right amount of time, in any situation, anyone can begin to feel comfortable again—or at least numb to the fear. He'd run until the edge of his panic dulled, until the adrenaline ebbed, leaving him hollow but steady. The field stretched around him, unseen and endless, and he exhaled, a steady breath that mixed with the air. He'd escaped the grasp, outrun whatever had touched him, and now he was here—alone, yes, but alive. The silence was familiar, a companion he'd known for years, and though it carried the echo of that groan, it didn't break him.

Then, suddenly, he felt a surge of confidence, a spark that flared in his chest and burned away the last of his trembling. What is darkness without hope? He turned around, his boots winding the grass, facing the direction he'd fled from. Why be afraid of what he couldn't see? The question rose, bold and defiant, cutting through the fog of fear that had held him. He'd spent years in the city cowering from shadows, from doubts, from a light that ignored him—years of running from the unknown, letting it rule him. No more. Whatever lurked in this dark, whatever had groaned and grabbed him, he'd confront it. He *must* know. He was done being afraid, done letting the unseen dictate his steps. He'd do anything to seek the truth, to face this beast—real or imagined—and strip it of its power over him. The shotgun had failed him, the city had failed him, but here, in this field, he'd take control, even if it broke him.

Bernie started walking back the way he'd come, his stride deliberate, his hands clenched into fists at his sides. The darkness was absolute, a wall he pushed through with every step, but he moved forward, his breath steady, his eyes straining against the black. He'd find it—the thing that had touched him, the source of the moan—and he'd face it, demand answers, end the mystery that gnawed at him. The field rustled around him and he felt a strange calm settle over him, a resolve forged in the fire of his fear. He walked, the silence thick and heavy, and noticed a peculiar thing: the landscape was getting ever so slightly brighter. It was subtle, a faint softening at the edges of his vision, as if the dark was thinning, as if the sun was rising at the slowest rate possible.

He stopped, his head tilting, his brow furrowing as he tested the change. The black wasn't as solid now—he could see the vague outline of his boots against the grass, a dim silhouette where before there'd been nothing. He lifted a hand, holding it inches from his face, and caught the barest hint of its shape, a shadow against the dark. The brightness grew, incremental but real, a creeping light that softened the void without revealing it fully. His heart thudded, a mix of confusion and something else —something lighter, something that lifted the weight from his chest. Hope washed over him, warm and unexpected, a tide that swept away the last of his terror. The field was changing, the night giving way, and though he didn't understand why or how, it felt like a sign, a promise that he wasn't lost.

He stood there and let that hope settle into him, fragile but real. The light he'd chased was gone, vanished when the moan had struck, but this new brightness was something else—a dawn, maybe, or a trick of this strange place. He didn't know what had grabbed him, didn't know where it was, but the growing light gave him courage, a thread to cling to in the dark. He took a step forward, then another, walking back toward the unknown, his eyes scanning the faint outlines that emerged around him. The grass stretched out, a shadowy sea, and the breeze carried a faint warmth now, a shift he couldn't explain. He was still alone, still blind to what lurked, but the fear that had paralyzed him ebbed, replaced by a quiet determination to face it, to find it, to know.

The brightness grew, slow and steady, painting the field in shades of gray—a world half-seen, half-hidden. He could make out the gentle roll of the land now, the waves of grass bending under the breeze, but no shapes moved, no figures loomed. The silence held, unbroken by another groan, and he wondered if he'd outrun it—or if it watched him still, waiting in the shadows that clung to the edges of this creeping dawn. He walked on, his boots thudding softly, his hands loose at his sides, and felt the hope strengthen with every step. The dark had been his prison, but now it was lifting, and though he didn't know what lay ahead— whether beast or truth or nothing at all—he moved toward it, a man reclaimed by a light he couldn't yet see.

14

Bernie continued his journey, the sun slowly rising on the horizon, its golden rays spilling across the field in a dance of light that took his breath away. It was the most beautiful sunrise he'd ever witnessed, a spectacle of color that wove together morning blues and purples, the hues bleeding into each other like paint on a canvas. The grass beneath him glowed the most vibrant green he could imagine, a lush, living carpet that stretched as far as the eye could see, rolling gently into the distance under the warming sky. The breeze brushed his face, carrying a faint sweetness now, a scent of earth and growth that felt alive, and he walked through it, his steps steady, his gaze fixed on the unfolding dawn. He didn't know exactly what direction he was traveling—east, west, it didn't matter here—but he could *feel* he was on the right track, a quiet instinct thrumming in his chest, guiding him forward.

Determined to find the mysterious creature that had terrified him before—the thing that had groaned in the dark, gripped his arm with unseen fingers—Bernie pressed on, hope and courage coursing through his veins like a river breaking free. The fear that had paralyzed him lingered, a shadow at the edges of his mind, but it was outmatched now by a fire he hadn't felt in much time—a resolve to face the unknown, to strip it bare and know it, no matter what it cost. He walked the grass parting before him in silent waves, and felt the world shift around him, subtle but real. Time, hunger, sleep—they didn't exist in this place, their absence a constant hum beneath his thoughts. He'd walked for hours, maybe days, without a pang in his stomach or a heaviness in his limbs, and he knew it was tied to this field, this endless expanse that defied the rules of the life he'd known.

The further he walked toward his goal, the brighter the sun became in the sky, its light intensifying with every step, a golden blaze that seemed to mirror the hope swelling inside him. It was almost as if the environment was a direct reflection of his soul—dark when he'd trembled, brightening as he found his courage, a living echo of his will. Bernie didn't know how this could be, how a place could bend to his heart, but it felt normal here, a truth woven into the fabric of this world. He tilted his head back, the warmth soaking into his face, and let the thought settle, a quiet wonder that steadied his stride. The field stretched on, vibrant and endless, and he moved through it, a man reborn in light, chasing a shadow he couldn't yet see.

Far away on the sky-blue horizon, Bernie noticed a dark cloud, a smudge of gray against the golden dawn, its edges ragged and heavy. His eyes narrowed, a flicker of recognition sparking in his chest—he knew, somehow, that he'd find the creature there. It was a certainty as real as the ground beneath him, a pull that drew him toward it like a magnet. A tinge of fear crept into his body, cold and honed, whispering memories of the moan, the grasp, the dark that had swallowed him whole. He paused, his breath shaking, but the courage and determination burning within him outweighed it, a steady flame that pushed the fear back. He changed direction, angling toward the cloud, his boots cutting a new path through the grass. The sun still rose, its light painting the field in gold, but the cloud loomed ahead, a promise of answers he couldn't turn from.

As Bernie walked, the cloud seemed to grow larger, swelling against the horizon, its gray deepening into a bruised purple that clashed with the dawn. The air thickened, the breeze turning damp and heavy, and he felt a single drop of water grace his forehead, cool against his skin. He stopped, tilting his face upward, and another fell, then another, until the sky darkened, the golden rays dimming under a veil of shadow. Fear enveloped his body, a sudden, suffocating wave that tightened his chest and quickened his pulse. The rain fell harder and faster, a relentless curtain that soaked his jacket, plastered his hair to his scalp, and ran in rivulets down his face. He stood there, the grass puddling beneath him, and felt anger start to replace the fear, a hot, bitter surge that rose in his throat. "Why me?" he thought, the words a silent scream against the storm. Why this place, this creature, this endless chase? He clenched his fists, the rain drumming against his knuckles, and continued walking, determination the only thing keeping him moving through the downpour.

Bernie knew he was close. The cloud hung low now, its edges swirling with mist, the rain a steady roar that drowned out the breeze. The field shimmered under the deluge, the grass bending under the weight of water, and he pressed forward, his boots squelching in the wet earth. The sun was gone, swallowed by the storm, and the world narrowed to shades of gray and black, a mirror of the city he'd left behind. His teeth clenched in the cold, his body drenched, but he didn't falter, didn't stop. The anger fueled him, a righteous fury at the unknown that had haunted him, and he scanned the horizon, his eyes stinging from the rain, searching for a sign, a shape, anything to confront.

Then it appeared—a black hooded figure, not more than one hundred steps from where he stood. It emerged from the mist like a shadow given form, its cloak billowing in the wind, its face hidden beneath the hood. Bernie stopped, poised for his next move, his breath a cork in his throat. The figure stood motionless, a dark silhouette against the storm, and he stared at it, the rain streaming down his face, his heart pounding with a mix of dread and recognition. Rage erupted in his soul, a hatred unlike anything he'd ever remembered feeling, a molten fury that surged through him and set his blood ablaze. Yet somehow, the hatred felt familiar, a deep, buried ember he'd carried without knowing —a memory, a wound, a truth he couldn't name.

Lightning struck the ground, a jagged bolt that split the sky and lit the field in stark white, and a red aura flared around the figure, a shimmering haze that pulsed with the thunder's roar. It raised its arms, the cloak flapping like wings, and laughed—a low, guttural sound that rolled through the storm, chilling and mocking, a voice that sank into Bernie's bones and twisted the rage tighter. Lightning struck again, closer now, the ground erupting in flame where it hit, a ring of fire that encircled the two of them like an arena of chaos. The heat licked at his legs, the flames crackling and spitting, their orange glow dancing in the rain-soaked dark. To a normal person, it would have been intimidating—a wall of fire, a figure wreathed in red, a storm that screamed—but Bernie was so full of anger and determination it was merely a mild distraction, a flicker at the edge of his vision. He didn't know where these feelings came from, this hatred that felt like home, but he felt they were justified, a righteous fire that matched the one around him.

Bernie stood there, the rain pounding against him, his fists clenched so tight his nails dug into his palms, drawing faint lines of blood that mixed with the water streaming down his hands. Tears welled in his eyes, hot and unstoppable, spilling down his already soaked face, blending with the rain until he couldn't tell them apart. The figure loomed ahead, its laughter fading into the storm's roar, its red aura pulsing like a heartbeat. He didn't know what it was—man, beast, shadow—but he knew it was the source, the thing that had groaned, that had grabbed him, that had haunted him across worlds. The flames flickered higher, the warmth a dull press against his skin, but he didn't flinch, didn't waver. His chest heaved, his breath ragged, and he took a step forward, then another, walking toward the hooded figure with a fury that burned brighter than the fire around them.

The rain lashed his face, the wind howled, and the ground trembled with each lightning strike, but Bernie moved through it all, a being possessed. The figure stood still, its arms raised, its presence a challenge he couldn't ignore. He didn't know what drove him—this rage, this need—but it felt right, a reckoning he'd waited for without knowing. The arena of flame tightened, the heat rising, the storm a chaotic symphony that matched the storm within him. He walked, his boots splashing through puddles, his eyes locked on the figure, tears and rain blocking his vision but not his purpose. He was close now and the hatred flared hotter, a familiar fire he'd carried through the dark, ready to meet its source.

15

Rain, lightning, fire, and so much hatred—the world around him was a maelstrom, a storm of chaos that roared in his ears and seared his skin. The rain lashed down in sheets, soaking him to the bone, the droplets stinging like needles against his face. Lightning split the sky, jagged bolts that lit the field in blinding flashes, illuminating the ring of flames that encircled him, their heat a constant press against his body. The air crackled with electricity, the scent of ozone and burning grass thick in his lungs, but none of it touched the fire inside him—a hatred so pure, so consuming, it drowned out everything else. He faintly remembered feeling this way before, flickers of anger from a life he couldn't fully grasp—arguments with Ellen over petty things, a sharp word to Sarah when patience wore thin—but never to this degree, never this raw, this all-encompassing. It was a rage that felt ancient, a beast unleashed from some deep, buried part of him, and it drove him forward, step by furious step.

None of it mattered—the storm, the fire, the rain-slicked grass beneath his boots. All that Bernie cared about now was reaching the figure in the black hood and destroying every single shred of its existence. It stood there, a dark silhouette against the chaos, its cloak billowing in the wind, its presence a taunt that fueled his hate. He didn't know why—who it was, what it was—but it was the source, the thing that had groaned in the dark, gripped his arm, haunted him across this endless field. He wanted it gone, obliterated, erased from whatever world this was, and he'd tear it apart with his bare hands if he had to. He moved forward, fueled by a hatred that burned hotter than the flames around him.

The black figure stood still in the lightning, its form unwavering as the storm raged. Bernie was close now—no more than a stone's throw away, the distance shrinking with every step, his boots splashing through puddles, his breath ragged and hot. Sweat, tears and water indistinguishable from each other on his face, but he saw it clearly: the hood hiding its face, the red aura pulsing around it, a glow that mocked him with every flicker. He was almost there, close enough to lunge, to strike, and then suddenly the world went black.

The shift was instantaneous, a void that swallowed everything—sight, sound, sensation. The rain stopped, the lightning vanished, the fire's heat snuffed out like a candle in a gust. He couldn't see or hear anything, the storm erased in a heartbeat, leaving him suspended in an abyss so complete it pressed against his skin like a living thing. His ears rang with silence, his eyes strained against the dark, but he knew the black-hooded being was still close by—an instinct, a certainty that thrummed in his bones. Bernie stood entirely still, straining his every sense for a feeling of anything other than dread and anger.

He stared into the abyss, his chest heaving, his fists ready to destroy. He couldn't see it, couldn't hear it, but it was there, and he stood poised, a coiled spring of rage waiting to snap.

Then, out of the blackness, a pair of red eyes opened right in front of him, glowing like embers in the void, inches from his face. The shock jolted through him, a spike of adrenaline that widened his eyes, but he was ready—ready to pounce, to end this. Without hesitation, Bernie threw a fist at the eyes with more power than he thought possible, a punch fueled by every ounce of hatred, every year of loneliness, every unanswered scream into the silence. His knuckles connected, a solid, bone-jarring impact that sent a shockwave up his arm, and the world erupted.

Red sparks filled the air, exploding outward from the point of contact, covering the landscape in an eerie, blood-red tone that bathed everything in a crimson haze. The black figure detonated with an awe-inspiring boom, a thunderous blast that shook the ground and hurled Bernie backward. He flew through the air, weightless and wild, his body tumbling as the force of the explosion ripped through him. An agonizing scream tore into his ears, a sound so piercing it cut through the chaos, and he knew it all too well—it was his own voice, raw and guttural, a cry of pain and triumph and something deeper he couldn't name. The world spun out of control, a whirl of colors and noise—red sparks, black void, flashes of lightning—and pain, dull and searing, radiated from his fist, his chest, his skull. Spinning, spinning, spinning, everything circled into a kaleidoscope of torment, and he couldn't tell up from down, reality from nightmare.

Finally, everything stopped.

The spinning ceased, the colors faded, and Bernie found himself lying flat on his back, the air knocked from his lungs. He tried catching his breath, his chest heaving, and blinked against a sudden, soft light that stung his eyes after the abyss. He was no longer in the field, no longer surrounded by rain and fire. He was on the sidewalk in front of a house in a suburban neighborhood, the concrete cracked and familiar beneath him, the edges worn smooth by time. He sat up slowly, his hands pressing against the ground, and looked around, a faint tremor running through him. He remembered this setting from long ago—it was *his* house, the one he'd lived in before everything happened, before the silence, before the city crumbled. The wooden railing, chipped and weathered, the screen door with its dented frame, the faint scent of cedar from the boards—it was all there, unchanged, a snapshot pulled from a life he'd lost.

Bernie felt his anger subside, the molten rage that had driven him cooling into a dull ache, replaced by a quiet, disorienting calm. He was no longer in an unfamiliar place, no longer adrift in a field of endless green or a storm of fire. He stood, his legs unsteady but holding, and ran a hand through his wet hair, the rain still clinging to him, his clothes heavy and cold. The sky above was clear, a dark blue tinged with the gold of late day, the sun low but warm. The neighborhood stretched around him—houses lined the street, their lawns trimmed, their windows glinting with light, a stillness that felt alive, not dead. He exhaled, a shaky breath that lingered in the air, and tried to grasp it—this shift, this return. Was it real? Had he punched the figure and woken here, or had the field been a dream, a fevered spiral of his mind?

Then, walking up the driveway, Bernie saw... himself.

He froze, his breath stopped, his eyes widening as the figure approached. It was him—Bernie, but not as he was now, soaked and trembling, a fist bloodied and pulsing from a fight in the dark. This Bernie wore a clean flannel shirt, jeans faded but intact, his hair neat and dry, his face unshaven but younger, tired but unlined by years of solitude. He carried a toolbox in one hand, the metal clinking softly with each step, and hummed a tune—something familiar and somewhat melancholy, a melody Bernie couldn't place but knew in his bones. The other Bernie didn't see him, didn't pause, just walked toward the house with a casual stride, the ease of a man who belonged here. Bernie stood on the sidewalk, his heart pounding, and watched himself climb the steps, the toolbox swinging lightly, the humming unbroken.

The screen door creaked open, and the other Bernie stepped inside, the sound of his boots on the hardwood floor echoing faintly before the door swung shut. Bernie remained outside, rooted to the spot, his hands trembling at his sides. The rage was gone, replaced by a flood of recognition, confusion, and something softer—longing, maybe, or grief. This was his house, his life, before the silence, before the light, before the field and the figure. He remembered the patio, the driveway, the way the sun slanted through the oak tree across the street, casting dappled shadows on the concrete. But seeing himself—another version, untouched by the years he'd endured—shook him to his core. Was this a memory? A trick? Or had he punched his way back to something real, something he'd lost?

He took a step toward the house, and paused. The air was warm, the neighborhood quiet, a faint breeze rustling the leaves overhead. He didn't know what waited inside—Ellen, Sarah, a life he couldn't prove, or just more shadows—but he felt the pull, a thread of familiarity that tugged at him. The pain in his fist lingered, a dull throb from the punch that had shattered the figure, and he flexed his fingers, the knuckles bruised and raw. The red sparks, the scream, the spinning—it had brought him here, to this moment, to himself. He didn't understand, couldn't piece it together, but he was here, and that was enough—for now.

Bernie stood there, tears drying on his face, the rain a fading memory, and stared at the door, the house, the driveway where he'd seen himself walk. The day nearing twilight, painting the sky with streaks of orange, and he felt the weight of it all—the hatred, the fight, the return—settle into something new, something he couldn't name.

PART 3

16

The light pulsed above, a faint heartbeat in the dusk, its glow softer now, less a call than a whisper, watching as it always had. The oak tree's shadow stretched long across the concrete, its branches gently waving in a breeze he couldn't feel, and the air carried a scent he couldn't place—cedar, maybe, or the ghost of something sweeter, something lost.

It was an eerie feeling at first, seeing yourself from the outside. Reflective, scary, ghost-like. Bernie watched himself walk up the patio, open the door, and enter his house—their house? The other Bernie moved with a tired familiarity, toolbox swinging at his side, humming a tune that felt like a memory of a memory, a ukulele riff he might have played on a night when the world still made sense. As he watched, he couldn't help but feel everything in this familiar place—memory?—felt oddly muted, stale, or blurred. Like his senses couldn't quite recall what was actually happening. The colors of the house were off, the white siding too gray, the red door too dull, as if the world had been drained of its vibrancy. The sounds—the creak of the patio boards, the rustle of leaves—were muffled, like he was hearing them through water. Even the air felt wrong, thick but empty, a void where sensation should have been. It was a contradiction of how he'd felt just moments ago in the green field with the hooded figure, where every blade of grass had been crystal clear, every lightning strike a jolt to his bones, every scream a release of the rage that had burned him alive.

What else could he do but follow himself inside the house? The light pulsed once, a faint encouragement or a warning, and he stepped forward, his boots scuffing the concrete —or so he thought, but there was no sound, no friction, just a hollow motion. Bernie had walked that old familiar path up his driveway and toward the door, the same path he'd taken a thousand times in a life he couldn't prove was real. The driveway was cracked, the lines deeper than he remembered, and the flowerbeds Ellen had once tended were gone, replaced by patches of dry earth. As his hand trembled over the doorknob, he tried to grasp the handle, but his fingers passed through it, the brass a mirage under his touch. A sense of dread crept in, cold and heavy, settling in his chest like a stone. Was he unable to feel this world? Change this world? All sense of control leaves when you can't feel. His hand hovered there, shaking, the doorknob solid but untouchable, a barrier he couldn't cross—not in a way that made sense.

Still, he wondered, *If I can't grasp the handle, can I pass through the door at all?* He tested the theory, leading his palm towards the door's surface. The wood looked real enough, its grain worn and peeling, but his hand fell right through, the sensation like pushing through fog, cool and weightless. His arm followed, then his shoulder, and with a stumble, the rest of his ghostly body passed through the doorway, the threshold wrinkling around him like a dream he couldn't wake from.

Bernie stumbled through the doorway just in time to see himself hanging his jacket on the coat rack inside the door. The other Bernie moved with a heaviness, his shoulders slumped, his steps slow, as if the day had wrung him dry. The jacket—a faded denim thing Bernie remembered wearing until the seams gave out —hung crooked on the rack, one sleeve brushing the floor. The entryway was just as he'd left it, or thought he had: the narrow table with its chipped paint, the mirror above it reflecting nothing but a blur, the faded rug Ellen had picked out at a flea market one summer. But it was all wrong, too—the table's edges were soft, the mirror's surface cloudy, the rug's pattern indistinct, like a photograph left too long in the sun.

He heard tiny muted footsteps running toward him and looked up. That's when he saw her. Sarah, or at least a figment of Sarah, not quite in focus but there all the same. She was so excited, her small frame a blur of motion, her hair a cascade that shimmered like it was caught in a haze. "Daddy! You're home! I missed you!" she cried, her voice a distant echo, bright but muffled, as if it came from the other side of a wall. She ran, arms outstretched, looking for a hug, her smile wide and unguarded, the kind of smile that had once been his whole world. Bernie watched himself—the other Bernie—as he ignored the child, opting to make his way to the sofa in the living room, seemingly exhausted from the day's work. The other Bernie didn't even glance at Sarah, his eyes fixed on the floor, his steps heavy as he sank into the cushions, head in his hands, a man too tired to see what was right in front of him.

17

Just as Bernie watched himself sit on the couch, ignoring the exuberance of his daughter, the room exploded in light.

FLASH

The living room dissolved, the muted colors of the house flaring into a blinding white, and when the glare receded, Bernie was still there, a ghost in his own memory, watching a scene unfold. Ellen stood in the kitchen doorway, her apron dusted with flour, her smile soft but tired as she told him a story—most likely of something Sarah had done while he was at work. Her voice was a distant hum, the words indistinct but the tone warm, a melody of a life he'd once held. The other Bernie sat at the dining table, a glass of water untouched in front of him, his eyes staring out into a void, a blank space where the window should have been. He wasn't engaged, didn't nod, didn't smile, just sat there, a statue of a man, his mind elsewhere, his heart closed to the woman who loved him. Ellen's story trailed off, her smile faltering, and she turned back to the kitchen, her shoulders slumping as she disappeared through the doorway, leaving the other Bernie alone with his emptiness.

Bernie's chest tightened, a hollow ache spreading through him as he watched the scene, his ghostly form hovering at the edge of the room, unable to speak, unable to change what he saw. He wanted to shout, to grab the other Bernie by the shoulders, to make him see Ellen, hear her, love her the way she deserved. But he was a shadow, a witness to his own failures, and the light pulsed again, a rhythm he knew too well, a heartbeat that had followed him through the city, the field, the storm.

FLASH

The dining room vanished, the white flare swallowing it whole, and when it faded, Bernie was outside, the backyard bathed in the golden light of a late afternoon. Ellen and Sarah were there, dancing around the yard, their laughter a bright, muffled echo that cut through the haze of the memory. Sarah spun in circles, her small hands clutching a dandelion, its seeds floating around her like tiny stars, her giggles a song that made Ellen laugh too, her face alight with a joy Bernie hadn't seen in years. They danced together, mother and daughter, their movements a blur of motion, their happiness a living thing that filled the yard with warmth. But the other Bernie was inside, napping on the couch, his arm slung over his eyes, the window framing him like a portrait of absence. He slept through their laughter, their joy, their life, a man who couldn't hear the music of his own family, who couldn't see the light they carried.

Bernie's shoulders knotted tight, though he felt nothing, his ghostly form trembling with a rage that wasn't rage, a grief that wasn't grief, but something deeper, something raw. He wanted to wake himself, to storm into the house, to drag the other Bernie outside and make him see, make him dance, make him live. But the light pulsed, its cadence faster now, a heartbeat that matched the ache in his chest, and the scene dissolved again, the laughter fading into silence.

FLASH

The backyard was gone, replaced by the dim light of a study, the walls lined with shelves that held books he'd never read, tools he'd never used. The other Bernie leaned over a desk, his attention completely taken by whatever he was working on—a blueprint, a sketch, a plan for a life he thought he needed. The desk lamp cast a harsh glow over his face, deepening the lines of exhaustion, the furrow of his brow, a man consumed by a task that meant nothing in the end. Sarah walked into the room, her small frame a blur at the edge of the memory, her voice a faint whisper Bernie couldn't hear. She asked something, her tone bright but hesitant, her hands clasped behind her back, waiting for an answer, for attention, for love. The other Bernie didn't look up, didn't speak, just waved a hand dismissively, his focus unbroken, his daughter unseen. Sarah's face fell, her smile fading, and she turned, her footsteps silent as she left the room, her disappointment a weight Bernie felt in his bones.

He wanted to scream, to shatter the desk, to make the other Bernie see what he was losing, what he was breaking with every moment of neglect. But he couldn't move, couldn't speak, his ghostly form trapped in the memory, his voice a whisper even to himself. The light pulsed, a warlike drumbeat now, a call he couldn't ignore, and the study dissolved, the white flare swallowing it whole.

FLASH

The room was gone, and Bernie was above it all, watching his house from a bird's-eye view, the roof a patchwork of shingles, the yard a square of green, the driveway a ribbon of gray. He saw it all unfold, day after day, a cycle of absence that played out in the muted colors of the memory. He watched as the other Bernie left for work each morning, his toolbox swinging at his side, his steps heavy with a purpose that kept him away. He watched as Ellen and Sarah lived without him, their days filled with small joys—Sarah drawing at the kitchen table, Ellen humming as she hung laundry, the two of them laughing in the yard while the sun sank low. He watched as the other Bernie returned each evening, his face a mask of exhaustion, his eyes blind to the life waiting for him, his hands empty of the love he could have held. Day after day, he ignored the very reason he lived, sinking into the couch, staring into the void, leaving Ellen and Sarah to dance alone, to laugh alone, to live alone.

The flashes pulsed just as the light had in the sky all this time, a rhythm that had followed him through the city's ashes, the field's endless green, the storm's fury. Each flash was a mirror, a memory, a truth he couldn't escape, and with each one, the realization hit Bernie like a wave, cold and heavy, absorbed into his chest, his gut, his soul. He created his own emptiness. Everything was right there—Ellen's love, Sarah's joy, a life he could have held, a warmth he could have felt—but he'd turned away, day after day, choosing the void over the light, the silence over the song. He'd built his loneliness with every missed moment, every ignored smile, every time he'd walked away from the family that needed him, that loved him, that was his whole world.

Bernie wanted nothing more than to shake himself awake, to make the shell of a man realize that connection was right there all along, that all he'd done was create his own loneliness. He was the creation of this emptiness, his own emptiness, a void he'd carved with his own hands, his own choices, his own blindness. He just needed to open his eyes, to see, to feel, to be there—but he hadn't, and now he was here, a ghost in a memory, watching the life he'd lost, the life he'd thrown away.

The flashes stopped, the white flare fading, and the house dissolved, the bird's-eye view collapsing into a void of light, the same light that had pulsed in the sky, that had led him through the dark, that had shown him his rage, his loss, his love. The living room returned, or a version of it, the colors muted, the edges soft, a dream within a dream. Sarah stood before him, her small form a blur of motion, her hair shimmering in the haze, her smile wide but fading, her voice a distant echo. "Where were you, Daddy?" she asked, her words cutting through the silence, sharp and clear where everything else was muffled, a question that broke him open, a wound that bled light.

Bernie's knees buckled, and he sank to the floor, his ghostly form passing through the rug, his hands reaching for Sarah, though he knew he couldn't touch her, couldn't hold her, couldn't answer her the way she deserved. "I was here," he whispered, his voice raw, the words a confession, a plea, a truth he'd buried too long. "I was here, but I wasn't. I'm sorry, Sarah. I'm so sorry."

The light pulsed, a final flare that swallowed the room, the house, the memory, and Sarah's form dissolved, her voice a fading echo—"Where were you, Daddy?"—as the whiteness returned, the void stretching on, the light hovering before him, its glow steady, its tempo slow, a heartbeat that matched his own. Bernie knelt there, tears streaming down his face, the light a mirror, a witness, a truth he couldn't escape. He'd created his own emptiness, his own silence, his own dark, and the light had watched, a reflection of the hope he'd buried, the love he'd lost, the man he'd failed to be. It didn't judge, didn't answer, just pulsed, a presence he could neither take nor give, a question he could only carry.

He stood, his hands falling open at his sides, the light before him, the whiteness around him, and let it be—not a path, not a promise, but a reflection of all he'd been, all he'd lost, all he'd learned. The melody faded, the echoes of Ellen and Sarah gone, and the light pulsed on, steady and open.

END

Bernie knelt in the void, the whiteness stretching on, a blank canvas that held the weight of his truth. The light pulsed before him, its glow slow and steady, a heartbeat that matched his own, a mirror of all he'd carried, all he'd lost, all he'd sought. Tears streamed down his face, hot against the cold of the void, and Sarah's voice echoed in his mind—"Where were you, Daddy?"—a question that had broken him open, a wound that bled light.

The light quickened its pulse and the whiteness shimmered, a fracture of green splitting the void like a tear in the fabric of nothing. The melody returned, a hum that carried the scent of grass, alive, a breeze that whispered through the emptiness. The green spread, the whiteness peeling away, and he was back in the field, endless and vibrant, its blades swaying in a wind he couldn't feel. The light hovered above, its glow softer now, a guide once more, leading him forward into the expanse. Bernie took a step, his legs drifting through the vastness—or so he imagined, there was no weight, no resistance, just the motion of walking, a ghost moving through a memory of a world. The field stretched on, infinite, its horizon a line he'd never reach, and the light pulsed, a steady rhythm that matched his steps and his entire being.

Ahead, the field shimmered, and the hooded figure appeared, standing still against the endless green, its form a shadow in the daylight, its cloak no longer wreathed in lightning or red sparks, but bare, a silhouette of absence. Bernie stopped, his breath catching, though he had no breath to catch, the memory of their fight flashing through him—the storm, the lightning splitting the sky, his fist striking the figure, the explosion of red, the scream that had torn from his throat. The rage didn't reignite, held back by the weight of his realization, the truth he'd seen in the house, in the flashes, in Sarah's question. The figure raised its arms, and the hood fell back, revealing a face that shifted—Ellen's warm eyes, Sarah's fleeting smile, his own weathered lines, then dissolving into a void that reflected everything and nothing.

The light pulsed, and the field rippled, the grass bending and rippling in silent waves, a dance of light and shadow that mirrored the journey he'd taken. The figure spoke, its voice a chorus—his, hers, theirs, a sound that wove through the air like roots threading the earth. "You've seen," it said, "what you made. What does it mean?"

Bernie's throat tightened, his voice rough as the words scratched their way out. "I don't know," he said, his mind a whirlwind. "I thought I hated you, the light, the silence. I thought I was alone because the world took everything!"

The figure tilted its head, the blur shifting, and the light pulsed behind it, sending ripples through the grass that shimmered, its green deepening then fading, then blooming again, a cycle of life and shadow that mirrored the storm in his chest. The field dissolved, and the city returned, its streets cracked and empty, the air thick with the scent of gasoline and ash. Bernie stood in the intersection where he'd poured the trails, the can at his feet, the match in his hand, striking it over and over, the flame refusing to catch, the silence swallowing his screams. The light pulsed above, a distant star in the sky, watching as he burned inside, his rage a fire that couldn't ignite, his loneliness a void he'd carved with every match, every scream, every moment he'd turned away from the life he'd had.

The city faded, and the field returned, endless and green, the light hovering closer now, its glow warm against his skin. He saw himself walking, his steps making a trail in the grass, the field stretching on, day after day, the light leading him forward, a guide he'd cursed, a hope he'd buried. He saw the shotgun in his hands, the barrel cold against his palm, the clicks hollow as he pulled the trigger, the silence laughing as he fell to his knees, the light pulsing above, a witness to his despair, a mirror to his dark. The field shimmered, and the storm came, the lightning splitting the sky, the rain soaking him through, the hooded figure laughing in the distance, its voice a taunt that drove him to strike, to fight, to scream. He saw his fist connect, the figure exploding into red sparks, his rage a storm that broke the dark, the light flaring in response, a reflection of his fury, his pain, his loss.

The field dissolved again, and the house appeared, the suburban patio under his feet, the screen door ajar, the scent of cedar thick in the air. He saw the other Bernie, the toolbox at his side, humming a tune he'd played on the ukulele, walking inside, ignoring Sarah's outstretched arms, her smile, her love. He saw the flashes—the dining table where he'd stared into the void, the couch where he'd napped through their laughter, the study where he'd dismissed Sarah's question, the bird's-eye view of a life he'd left behind, day after day, creating his own emptiness, his own silence, his own dark. Sarah's voice echoed—"Where were you, Daddy?"—and the light pulsed, its rhythm a heartbeat that matched his own, a mirror of the truth he'd seen, the loneliness he'd made.

The house faded, and the field returned, the hooded figure still before him, the light hovering above, its glow steady, its presence never judging. "What does it mean?" the figure asked again, its voice a whisper carried on the breeze that rustled the grass.

Bernie sank to his knees, the grass cushioning his descent, his tears falling again, hot and silent, tracing paths down his weathered face. "I took everything… It means, I was the silence," he said, his voice breaking, raw with the weight of it. And the realization induced more rage, "I wanted to burn the city because I couldn't burn the nothing inside me! I shot at the dark because I couldn't stop myself! I walked the field because I couldn't stop running from what I'd lost! I fought you because I was too much of a coward to fight myself! And the house… my family…" Bernie's rage turned to grief, "I made the emptiness there, long before the silence came. I was alone because I chose to be."

The figure stepped closer, its form softening, its blur fading at the edges, blending into the light that pulsed behind it.

"I am what you see," it said, its voice a chorus again, soft and layered. "The light you cursed, the dark you fought, the hope you buried, the rage you burned. I am the mirror of your soul, the echo of your steps, the shadow of your silence. What do you see now?"

Bernie looked up, the light's glow warm against his skin, matching the heartbeat he felt in his chest, a presence he'd chased, cursed, fought, and finally seen. He saw the city, the field, the house, all of it a canvas of his journey—dark with his despair, bright with his will, stormy with his rage, muted with his loneliness. The light had been there through it all, a witness, a guide, a mirror, reflecting his hope when he'd lost it, his rage when he'd burned, his love when he'd forgotten, his emptiness when he'd turned away. It wasn't an answer, not a path, but a truth, a presence that held everything he'd been, everything he'd lost, everything he'd found.

"I see me," he said, his voice steady now, the tears drying on his face. "I see the man who burned, who walked, who fought, who lost. I see the man who loved, who failed, who left. I see the light I hated, the light I needed, the light I am."

The figure's form dissolved fully into the light, its voice fracturing, carried on the wind that swayed the field. "You see," it said, and the grass rippled—bending, fading, blooming—a dance of light and shadow that pulsed with the glow. The field stretched around him, endless and alive, the city a memory in the distance, the house a hum on the wind, a shadow of before. The light pulsed brighter, its warmth seeping into the grass, through the air, into him—a weight, a question, a looking glass. It flared once more, washing over him, through him, a final reflection of all he'd carried, all he'd sought, all he'd become.

Bernie stood fully upright for the first time in a long time. The field was his soul—dark with his despair, bright with his will, stormy with his rage, alive with his truth. The light was its heart, a mirror he'd cursed, chased, fought, and finally seen, a presence that had watched him since the silence fell, a reflection of the man he'd been, the man he was. The city, the field, the house—they were all him, all part of the journey, the echo of everything he'd lived, everything he'd lost, everything he'd found. He took a step forward, the grass shifting under his weight, the light pulsing on, steady and open, a question or a truth, a mirror for what he saw in it: hope, hate, love, loss, himself.

The field held still, glowing under a sky of gold and blue, a beautiful canvas of endless colors. The light remained, a heartbeat in the air, a presence he could carry, a truth he could bear. Bernie stayed there unmoving through time, a man at the edge of light and shadow, his story an echo of everything, his journey a mirror for the beholder.

About the Author:

C.D. Reeves lives in Montana with his wife, two kids, and two dogs who-along with the kids-probably think they rule the place.

When he's not writing, he's playing music (he's always been an avid-lover of his local music scene), digging into video games, or mulling over big thoughts, usually with a cup of tea in hand.

World Gone Quiet took ten years to brew, born from a restless, curious mind that's always dodging the quiet.

www.ingramcontent.com/pod-product-compliance
Lightning Source LLC
Chambersburg PA
CBHW030539130626
46552CB00006B/2335